Place with no Name

Place with no Name

Catriona Tawse

ISBN: 978-1-912270-30-9

Published by:
Ross-shire Writers
41 Urquhart Road
Dingwall
IV15 9PE

Printed by *For the Right Reasons*

The stories in this collection are composed entirely of works of fiction.
No resemblance to any real persons, alive or dead, or actual events, is
intended. Any such resemblance is entirely coincidental. Familiar place
names in Scotland are used to provide a local context for the tales herein.

Contents

ACKNOWLEDGMENTS

This varied collection of stories links together characters that emerged from my imagination over a ten year period. I have located them in a *Place with No Name* which many readers will recognise as a typical West Coast Village...or is it?

I would like to thank *Ross-Shire Writers* for their support and encouragement in helping me complete this project. Our Chairman Reg Holder has been instrumental in keeping the goal of 'getting published' alive. I want to thank Sandra and Louise in particular for smoothing the way by taking on the task of editing and dealing with all the technicalities needed to get the stories from my laptop to publication.

I hope you get as much pleasure reading these stories as I did from writing them.

Thanks also go to *For the Right Reasons* for their professional service in producing and printing this little volume.

Catriona Tawse (MacRitchie)
Strathpeffer, September 2018

Safe from the Storm

There had been no warning. Nothing on the charts and forecasts which followed the evening news. Not a sign in the sky. The sudden destructive onslaught of this late October wind baffled the credulity of those with years of experience at sensing change.

On his croft old Calum Gillies often struggled on the calmest of days yet he now set to his tasks with determination. Quickly he ushered the indignantly clucking hens into the wooden shed, their feathers ruffling in unbecoming disarray as he strained to hold open the door. His milk cow and the two calves he had then found on the west side with their backs to the wind, they now stood ill at ease in the byre yanking at tufts of hay, eyes rolling in panic at each savage roof-rattling gust. The old man trudged round checking all was secure, pausing for a moment behind the peat stack to catch his breath before making for the shelter of his back door.

Its thatched roof long since converted to slate, Calum's little house crouched low in the shelter of a ridge of rocky scrub and bracken. The few poor trees out front stooped in submission to the prevailing north-westerlies but the shingly cove beyond the machair lay curved in the sheltering arm of an out-thrust headland. Bowed by his years and the forceful gale he stooped through the porch reflecting quietly as he usually did that his dear wife Mary was no longer there to welcome him home. Unchanging in her devotion her greeting had always been 'Safe from the storm' even though the day had been untroubled. Sadly the growth they found inside her head was not to be cured.

"Safe from the storm, thanks be to the Lord." Calum whispered as he stretched his slippered feet to warm at the peat fire. The appetising smell of broth reheating on the range drifted through as he rubbed the ache in his crippled leg, knowing he would need a while to recover from the efforts of the afternoon. It was growing harder to get even as far as the village shop but he lived in a place where neighbours looked out for one another. The old sheepdog Cuillin slumbered and twitched on the fireside rug as Calum dunked a thick wedge of crusty loaf into his soup.

Outside the wind screeched and blew explosively in orchestrated cacophony. Windows and slates rattled with demented percussion and roaring blasts in the chimney threw billows of peaty reek back into the room. For a moment he could barely see across to the dresser where a row of family photos took pride of place, a tangible link with a happy past. There was himself and Mary, posing formally at the wedding of their elder son John. Gordon, their other boy, had been lost at sea when the trawler went down with all hands. His mother had never recovered from the anguish of that dreadful day. Daughter Annie in nurse's uniform smiled out from another frame and Wilma, who he had to admit was his favourite, waved cheekily from the pillion of a one-time boyfriend's motorbike. Now she was so far away living in Canada with her husband Tom. Just recently a letter had come with the glad news that their daughter Louise was expecting her first child very soon. Calum could hardly believe he was going to be a great grandfather; it saddened him to think that Mary would not be there to share such a special event. The knitting needles would have been very busy. He smiled to himself.

A shattering crash from outside made the old man start in alarm. Setting down his empty plate he pushed his feet back into the boots and hobbled to the door, torch in hand. It would be slates off, he reckoned, shining a beam out of the door. He blinked in disbelief and shook his head, almost certain he could see lights in the cove. Surely not a boat; who would venture out on a night like this? Without hesitation he pulled on his jacket and with his crook for support he set out along the uneven path, the collie at his heels.

As he neared the shore Calum saw a distress flare soar briefly above the bulk of a vessel wallowing in the thrust of each wave which forced it towards the rocky foreshore. He could not determine over the fiendish buffeting of the gale if it was still under power but he could distinguish through the spray that it was one of these extravagant cabin cruisers so much favoured by the well-to-do.

'Whatever possessed them in this weather?' Calum wondered. The storm HAD been sudden, he admitted, maybe they had tried to run before it to this tiny bay in hope of shelter. As the doomed craft piled hard against the rocks pathetic cries for help came faintly through the wind's relentless howl.

Calum was not to know that the whim of the selfish woman on board had brought them all to such peril. She would have the baby before Christmas, she had raged, and that would be an end to their sea-going jaunts for far too long. Worn down by petulant nagging the husband had given in, and along with their eleven year old son they had put to sea in almost a million pounds worth of sleek power, top of the range from that year's prestigious Boat Show.

Intent on giving what aid he could Calum tried to ignore the sharp pain shooting through his leg as he scrambled over the rocks.

'God is our refuge and our strength,' he murmured, feeble and alone against the might of the wind. As he cast around with the light of his torch he watched in horror as a small boy was flung ashore almost at his feet. "Please help us," he gasped, the words scarcely audible. "My father, my mother. They are in the water." He stumbled unsteadily out of the water's reach. The next breaker tossed up the figure of a heavily built man who clutched his hands to his heaving chest, his breath coming in noisy gasps.

"My wife... my wife..." was all he managed before falling still. Stretching out with his crook Calum tried desperately to catch the woman's arm as she floated forward. She was a large lady too, he observed, then with a jolt he realised that her near-drowned body was heavy with child just like his own granddaughter Louise on the other side of the world. That thought gave him renewed strength as he hauled and strained to bring this unknown woman to what he hoped was safety. One last heroic heave got her onto a ledge where she lay motionless and silent.

The brave old man had done all he could. Giddy with pain and despair he felt his own exhausted body sink among the slippery stones, felt himself merging comfortably into one with them. And as his life dwindled all fear and sorrow faded for he could see his beloved Mary. Closer and closer she came, smiling to him, her face wreathed in the very light of God's breath. Holding out her arms she called softly, 'Safe from the storm ... safe from the storm.' His tired old heart slowed to its last beat as a sea-spray burst of myriad stars soared him to death's vast beyond.

Soaked and shaking the boy clung to the rough black coat of the whimpering collie.

The storm raged on around them.

Water under the Bridge

She was pleased that it was her cousin Ishbel who had broken the news and not the gloomy minister or that old busybody MacSween from the shop. Annie had just come off night shift when the phone rang. Later she recalled saying she'd organise a flight that afternoon and hire a car in Inverness but in reality the day passed in a blank daze. Her poor old father had died a lonely death on the edge of the shore trying to help people he did not even know.

So typical, she thought, putting others before himself. It had been he who insisted she carried on with her nursing career after her mother died and truth be known she had been all too happy to take him at his word that he would 'manage fine'.

To her relief Ishbel and her husband had seen to the arrangements for the burial that Wednesday leaving Annie time to prepare for the formalities which would be observed. There would be customary drams and heartfelt expressions of sympathy back at the house with women folk in the kitchen keeping the teapots full.

Her brother John had arrived the night before, emphasising selfishly how hard it was for him to get away, the implicit suggestion being that his work in his father-in-law's firm was of greater importance. Drusilla his wife had flatly refuse to accompany him, she did not see the point of funerals; when you were dead you were dead and that was an end to it. Sister Wilma had been understandably unable to fly home from Vancouver where her daughter Louise was expecting her first child any day. As the old folk often said, when one life goes another comes to take its place, a small comfort to the grieving family.

The Reverend MacIntyre had spoken sincere words of tribute from the pulpit, moving many to tears. Miss Mason from the school had played the wheezy harmonium with great feeling. Willing shoulders had taken turns to carry the coffin up the slope to its final resting place. Calum Gillies had been much loved and respected in the community.

In the numb aftermath Annie had mechanically cleaned and tidied the croft house, reluctant to remove all traces of the old man's existence but realising the necessity if she was to have the place put up for letting. Several times she climbed the shaky ladder to the loft to stow away things which held dear memories. Treasured family photos she could take with her while Ishbel had offered to store items too heavy for her flight allowance.

"Who knows?" Ishbel had said. "Perhaps you'll come back yourself when it's time to retire."

Later in the week she decided it was time to collect the collie from Dougal Kennedy the coastguard's house where his wife Rhoda had cared for both the dog and the wee boy left behind after his parents had drowned. Any resentment she felt toward the survivor disappeared as soon as she saw him sat by the window, wan and withdrawn, stroking the dog's head.

"I hear you have been looking after Cuillin," she said softly. "That was very kind. I can see he likes you."

She crouched down beside the wooden seat to be on his level and was rewarded by the faintest trace of a smile.

"I don't know if Uncle Arnold will let me have a dog," he confided, tugging on the sleeve of a much too large jersey. "I don't really know Uncle Arnold at all. He'll be coming for me tomorrow." He turned his face away in case this nice lady might see his tears. Annie felt such a pang of pity for the poor lost soul, all the familiar things in his life so suddenly gone.

"Well … Gerald, isn't it?" The boy nodded. "Would it be all right if I asked you to take care of Cuillin for one more night, just till your uncle gets here?"

Gerald slipped off the bench and put his arm round the dog's neck.

"Yes please, I'd like that very much."

Rhoda came through with cups and biscuits on a tray.

"You'll be pleased to know Roddy is doing well for himself out in Manitoba; it's near ten years since he went over and never a word of coming home."

"Goodness, is it as long as that?" Annie wondered if Rhoda had been aware of the fancy she had once had for her quiet young brother. She held out her hand for the cup.

Luckily the big hospital had been understanding about extended time off. It was obviously going to be left to Annie to attend to matters regarding what had been their family home. Warmly wrapped up against the crisp chill of the November day she set off with the dog for a brisk walk to think things over. It was obvious how much Cuillin felt the loss of his master, constantly sniffing and searching and looking up with sad brown eyes. Perhaps later she would take up some of the many offers of help but for now she wanted to breathe the familiar tang of sea and reek of peat, a sharp contrast with her life in a bustling city.

She stopped at the bridge, a familiar meeting place in the innocent days of youth when she would persuade her pals to hang about a while in case Roddy Matheson might pedal past on his way home. They met socially at dances and ceilidhs but he scarcely had a word to say for himself. Even after leaving for nursing college she never quite put him out of her mind – until recently when she met Finbar, but it was early days there.

Leaning back on the stony parapet she watched Johan Matheson, now Fraser, coming along the flat road with her three year old twins, Evie, pushing a dolly's pram which seemed to have an engine attached judging by the accompanying noises while Duggie forged ahead on a silver scooter. She called out a greeting as Johan came nearer. 'She could have been my sister-in-law'. Annie smiled to herself. They chatted about village things: who'd got married, who might be thinking about it, who was expecting. Annie forgot about her own sadness for a bit.

"What have you in mind for the croft?" Johan asked bluntly. "Leave the dog alone." She chided the boisterous pair who were trying repeatedly to get Cuillin to give a paw.

"It would be best if I could lease it to someone who would use the good ground my father put so much work into. If nobody local is interested I'll put it in the paper. Willie John would take the cow and her calves and the hens will go to Ishbel, she's been such a help to me. And she always looked out for Dad once he got a bit less able on the legs. Come the spring the sheep can go to the sales; some of the crofters have said they will take care of that."

"What about the dog?" Johan knew her own brood would maul the poor brute to death. "A quiet retirement for him somewhere?"

"Your sister will take him back. He got a bit used to being there after Dad …" Annie fumbled for a hanky. Recovering, she grinned at Johan.

"Here's a surprise for you. I think I might have found a fellow after all this time and me heading fast towards forty!"

"Get away with you; it's high time – tell me more."

"Not much to tell yet. His name's Finbar and he's from Galway. He's a self employed painter and decorator and he plays the uillean pipes."

Johan laughed. "You always did like the music – and he'd be a useful man to have about the place! We'd all wish you well but my goodness lassie, why on earth could you not have made a go of it with our Roddy. He always thought you were the one for him but he was too shy to do anything about it. I suspect you had a notion for him as well. And no, he never married, just in case you're wondering."

Annie's face went quite pink. "Och maybe once upon a time but it's too late; we've gone our separate ways. No point thinking what might have been. It's as they say all water under the bridge now."

She turned away and dropped a loose stone into the burn below, watching the ripples spread in the peaty brown water.

Settling in

There was no doubt about it. Lavinia folded the final missive from the Fordham and Dudley Law firm and returned it carefully to its thick cream envelope.

"We are rich." Her voice was a mere whisper. With somewhat less restraint her sister Beryl echoed the statement.

"Oh good old Daddy, God bless him. I always thought he would see us all right even though we weren't always on the best of terms."

Good old Daddy, Edward Ambrose Eddington, senior partner in a well-established company of property developers, had also been an astute player of the stock market and even after all taxes and duties had been cleared the sums deposited in his daughters' bank accounts had been staggeringly generous .

"There's so much we could do." Lavinia pushed the plunger into the cafetière filling the kitchen with a tantalising aroma. "We've always been comfortably off but this could be life changing. Anything we've dreamed of in the past can if we want become reality."

"No more corsets for me!" beamed Beryl, smacking her lips appreciatively, croissants had never tasted so good. For fifteen years she had been with 'Modes for Madame' as an advisor for and fitter of reliable undergarments for the amply proportioned lady, a description which was perfectly applicable in her own case. The more studious Lavinia had been a behind the scenes assistant to the elderly and recently retired proprietor of an antiquarian bookshop, working out of interest rather than financial necessity.

"Should we go swanning round the world on one of these cruise liners on a year long voyage or settle for that Highland hideaway we've so often spoken about?"

Beryl would happily have settled for the second option and was startled to hear her sister remark that there was nothing to stop them from doing both.

"We might pay a visit to the travel agents for starters and for the other matter we should consult Daddy's old firm. I suppose Highland properties are a bit outside their territory but there's every chance they will have contacts up north. I'll give Bob Drysdale a ring; he was one of Daddy's protégés from the early days."

"That's all for today." Jimmy the Post placed the bundle of mail on the shop counter. Hector MacSween glanced at it briefly, it would keep till later.

"How's your new neighbours settling in?" he enquired. The recent arrival of two clearly well-to-do English ladies into Ian Willie's old croft at number 37 had been the subject of much curious speculation in the village.

"They've just brought home a brand new Jeep Cherokee, a monster of a thing. It will cost a small fortune to keep it on the road. The garage folk will be pleased enough." The postman grinned. "Father had the spyglass on them yesterday afternoon. One of them had the Shetland pony on a rope and the other one was giving its tail a good going over with a brush."

"Hope the fat one doesn't get on its back; the poor thing would collapse," chortled Hector. His wife appeared through the door which connected the shop to the house.

"Is that you men making fun of the English ladies again?" she reached under the counter for the pricing gun. "They're perfectly nice people. Miss Lavinia has given us a standing order for some magazines I'd never heard of – not cheap I can tell you – and shouldn't we be glad they are coming here at all for their messages and not going up to town like some I could mention." The gun clicked into rapid action on the tops of tins of beans.

"Miss Beryl, Miss Lavinia, they sound like something from Queen Victoria's day." Jimmy was amused. "They'll maybe drop the formalities once we get to know them better – if they're here long enough." He opened the door and stood aside, his face reddening.

"Morning Miss Lavinia, how are you today? It's nice to see a bit of sunshine."

"Yes." Lavinia nodded in agreement, memories of their world cruise fading along with the suntans they had acquired. Getting the croft had been far from straightforward; some officialdom called the Crofting Commission had been involved in lengthy negotiations with the Eddington family solicitors.

"I'm away to the house with the letters," Hector announced. He thought his wife looked a bit tired; she was always on the go. "I'll put Peigi through to give you a hand."

Both daughters were involved in the family business, the elder Dolina, or Dollag as she was more often known, had been sent on a

9

book keeping course. Peigi admitted to having little head for figures and was content to take a turn behind the counter.

"I really only came in for these delicious oatcakes, Mrs. MacSween." Lavinia set down the wire basket to which she had also added a sliced brown loaf and a pot of honey. This was so much friendlier than an impersonal call to Fortnums. Two ladies she had not seen before came in. Introductions were made and pleasantries exchanged before Lavinia backed towards the exit unsure in her mind if Highland folk were on the whole amicably curious or simply downright nosy.

The late-November rain battered relentlessly on the triple glazed windows of number 37. Beryl's blinds and curtains had been closed since mid afternoon. She'd shut the hens in early and was giving Flossie an extra armful of hay, both of them half deafened by the screams of the wind as it did its best to remove the corrugated iron roof. These days she was seldom out of her waxed jacket and the green wellingtons, the pristine appearance of which in 'The County Set' had given no hint of the realities of rural living. The Mcfuel lorry had topped up their tank only yesterday. Installing the Aga had been the best idea ever. She splashed across the yard to the shelter of the back porch. This evening, after Lavinia's hotpot and home made crumble had been disposed of, the intention was to sit down and give the immediate future serious consideration over a small glass of sherry.

Lavinia was watching the weather forecast which promised more wind, more rain and wintry showers on higher ground. The sisters had agreed that they would try not to be beaten by the elements. The first line of defence had been the unstoppable 4x4 and then the acquisition of a very large deep freeze. Mrs MacSween in the shop had been helpful with advice about torches and candles in case of power failures. Possible delays in the postal services could also be expected, nor would the ferry always be able to keep its normal timetable.

Right now they felt that the croft needed more animals. A retired greyhound awaited collection from the re-homing centre and the cats Agatha and Christie (an early gift from the family at the garage) were at that moment polishing off their bowls of Kittievitties in the kitchen. The one small pony alone in its big shed deserved company, the pros and cons of which now had to be weighed with care.

Part of the fence had fallen down where Lavinia had inexpertly reversed the jeep; someone was coming from the town to repair it. Perhaps some time next week, he had said. That odd old man with the bicycle had offered, but not wishing to impose they had declined with thanks. Sheep were ruled out anyway – Beryl didn't like the way they stared at her and they were far too flighty. Would a cow be more manageable? They could get one without horns. But think of the sheer size of a cow! Which of them would be able to milk it? They exchanged alarmed glances. Lavinia unstoppered the decanter again and poured generous measures.

"Perhaps we could try goats; experts say their milk is very healthy." Beryl made a lap in her tweed skirt for Christie who jumped up, rewarding her by immediately stabbing his claws into her plump leg.

"They are smaller and less threatening than a cow." Lavinia warmed to the idea, savouring her third sherry. "If it's not too stormy tomorrow we could drive over to the farm. I've heard folk speak highly of Farmer MacDonald's knowledge of livestock. No need to decide at once but I'm sure he could give us some good advice."

Beryl's face glowed rosily in the firelight. "Yes, and call in at the school on the way back. You know how we spoke of putting on a Christmas party for the pupils and their mums and dads. Some really festive food and gifts for all the children – we could order the lot from Harrods. I imagine the teacher would be thrilled with the idea."

At that time neither of these well intentioned benefactors had met the formidable Miss Mason . . .

Out of Control

The class drifted in for registration. There was just a week to go till the end of term, for some the end of schooldays altogether.

"Isabella Anderson! What on earth are you wearing?" Miss MacLachlan's sharp voice silenced the chatter.

"It's a boob tube Miss. Do you like it? I got it from a charity shop. You should get one for the summertime Miss."

Bella slouched to her seat. It had taken only a few seconds to shove the top down her jeans when the elderly volunteer was arranging coloured T-shirts on the rail.

"Have you nothing else to put on? It looks so..." the teacher hesitated over the word 'tarty'. This girl had been a constant troublemaker.

"Suppose I might have a sweatshirt in my locker." Bella muttered. She well knew the reaction her latest fashion statement would provoke; winding Miss MacLachlan up was almost too easy. She sauntered out of the room as the teacher began to call out names.

Bella had no intention of hurrying back to that class. She could head straight for Dopey Donaldson's Modern Studies in Room 14 in about ten minutes but first she fancied a fag, gasping for one since she had hurried off the late-running school bus where the driver enforced the no smoking rule in spite of her flashing the boob tube. 'He's quite nice looking for an old man,' Bella thought, swinging her way to the rear seats. The driver was twenty five.

Neilly Murray appeared from a side door, late as usual. He sidled up to Bella with what he imagined was a sexy grin.

"Got any fags on you Neilly?" Bella's smile was as false as her fingernails.

"Might have." She wriggled about, knowing he was ogling her skimpy top.

"What'll you do if I give you a fag? Can I have a feel? Show's your ..."

Bella grabbed his arm and steered him back out the side door.

"Later," she promised with a sly wink. "Cm'on Neilly, hurry up; we'll be in for it if we're late for Dopey's".

In the staff room later the subject turned as it so often did to Isabella Anderson, Miss MacLachlan loudly deploring the state of her apparel and the lack of regard the girl had for authority.

12

"Thank heaven she's leaving this year. Four more days. I don't suppose she's had any thought of work." She dropped her squeezed teabag into the bin.

"Perhaps she isn't entirely to blame." Lizzie Hendry taught art and her more liberal ways were not generally shared.

"Her mother does what she can, worn out with keeping the family together and trying to work the croft while that disgusting creep she married props up the bar in the Caley eyeing up anything in a skirt." Lizzie was not about to admit that she had herself once been on the receiving end of one of his chat-up lines. She'd come close to putting the knee on him but managed to walk away with her dignity intact.

"What do you expect? He's not from around here," another voice broke in. "They say he knocks her about a bit and all."

A bell signalled the end of breaktime. Mr Donaldson sighed as he replaced the lid on the biscuit tin. Retirement for him was still a long six years away.

Lizzie Hendry paused on her way to the next class to make sure that the posters for end of term disco had not been embellished with anything unpleasant. The staff's presence at these events was not optional. Nowadays you needed all round vision and the sensitivity of a bloodhound to keep track of the over-stimulated youngsters. Drink was always a problem even with the closest supervision.

The school gym looked quite festive by Friday's final bell. The DJ decks had been set up and a band of young hopefuls calling themselves 'Petrol Shed' had been enlisted to play in the first half, both the drummer and the bass player affecting a casual swagger as they carried their gear across the floor where not so very long ago they had reluctantly performed squat thrusts and press-ups.

In the girls' toilets the air was heavy with anticipation and cheap perfume. Bella was a sensation, flouting all conventional dress rules.

"You look like a witch," giggled her best mate Jody. "Nobody else would have the nerve to come here wearing black from head to toe. I love your fish-nets."

"Did you come on your broomstick?" asked another girl sneeringly, herself clad in an unobtrusive blouse and skirt in shades of pink.

Bella was applying black mascara lavishly on her kohl-ringed eyes. There was only so much she could get off with before setting

13

out. Her mother had been anxious about the black ensemble, her father as usual unavailable for comment. She produced a half bottle of vodka from her bag.

"Time to get the party started," she unscrewed the metal top and glugged some down. Jody and the others crowded round. Miss All-in-Pink swept through the exit door.

"I'll have to find a good hiding place." Bella put the lid back on. "That stuck up cow will be away to tell. Go on you lot, out of here."

As far as school functions went the disco was not bad at all. Petrol Shed had played loudly if erratically and the DJ had plenty of popular hits. Robbie Williams was every young girl's dream.

"I'm fainting with the heat," Bella explained to the dishy young science teacher on door duty. She had not been in his class. You needed brains for that kind of stuff.

"OK then but don't be long; the janitor will be doing his rounds any time soon."

Fat lot she cared; it was getting a bit boring anyway. Wee boys like Neilly Murray did not interest her, but oh my god he had followed her out.

"Bella, Bella," he whispered urgently. "There's a pal of mine wants to see you, over here."

A rusting white LDV van was parked up. It belonged to a notorious local hard man Finn Finlayson, otherwise known as The Bradan.

"What's he want?" Bella was intrigued; he was older than her and his bad reputation somehow gave him an added appeal. She got in the van without a backward look at Neilly.

"Fancy a spin down to the shore?" Finn already had the engine running and was pulling away before she could say aye or no. This was fun, she was sure there would be more to come. The bass speakers thudded as Ozzy and Black Sabbath powered through 'Paranoid'. Finn casually lit two cigarettes and passed one to Bella. She could smell whisky on him and hoped he had more with him.

Next morning nursing a raging headache Bella tried to piece together what had happened. Warmed and confused by the whisky she had not resisted the Bradan's charm and sweet talk. He had almost kissed the face off her while his octopus hands roamed in exciting directions.

14

"More comfortable in the back," he had said. Too right. There was a small lumpy mattress on the floor, something smelled like wet sheep, empty lager bottles clinked as they climbed in. The next bit had been rather hazy and hasty, nothing like what she'd read about in 'Go for it!' magazine. Only heavy metal had played and the earth had remained quite still. There had been no meaningful glances, no mention of love. She had felt nothing other than a passing soreness and a sticky damp. He'd driven her to her road end and roared off without so much as a goodnight kiss. Lurching a lot she followed the track, her bare legs whitely pale in the semi dark of a Highland summer night.

It was nearing the end of Autumn when Bella and her patient mother sat on a bench outside Sadie Graham's Wednesday clinic in the little village hall. Even before the blue-uniformed District Nurse called her in Bella knew for sure what the answer would be. Perhaps Finn would marry her; it was still considered the decent thing to do. And what about names? She fancied Robbie if it was a boy. Whitney would be nice for a girl . . .

Out of the Frying Pan

"Are you going to do the right thing by the girl?" his mother asked, recalling her own past shame and hastily arranged marriage.

"Why should I?" Finn growled. "Don't you believe I was the only one that went with her; she's good with her lies."

"You'd better hope Calum Nandag sees it that way. He won't want his family name taken down. Bella's a fine strong lassie, you could do a lot worse."

Finn barged out of the room, banging the door so hard that a picture fell off the wall. Mairead gently picked it up. It was of herself and Wattie Finlayson on the top step of the church more than twenty years ago. The glass was in one piece but the cord had broken. She sighed. So much else had been broken since that day including her heart and the vows made to her.

The fourth and last and largely ignored daughter of Kenneth Morrison the stonecutter she had been plain, plump and eager to please, an easy target for Wattie's predatory advances. Nobody was more surprised than herself when he roughly agreed he would marry her. But, he had told her, she would have to be prepared for him being away from home months at a time. He was a roustabout on a North Sea drilling rig. Mairead thought that sounded important enough and was willing to go along with whatever he said. She didn't know all that much about him except that he belonged to Aberdeen and had relations there. None of them were invited to the wedding.

Wattie had been off shore when their son was born. Mairead had a difficult time but her mother and sister were there with advice and practical help. There was no way of knowing when her man would be home and the birth had to be registered. The one happy distraction in her otherwise unglamorous life was her passion for films and she made up her mind to name the boy after a much admired movie hero playing the tough guy who overcame all odds ending up with a bloodied face and his clothes in tatters.

Going to school for the first time was a big step in a five year old boy's life. He had seldom seen his father, and his mother had compensated by being somewhat over-protective. The teacher called the register in alphabetic order.

"Roderick Cameron, Mary-Anne Cunningham, Norman Duncan, Sylvester Finlayson." Someone sniggered loudly. Miss Mason said "Be silent," and continued. "Dolina Mackintosh, Christine Morrison…" until all fifteen pupils were accounted for.

"We will say the Lord's Prayer. All stand. Eyes closed. Our Father…"

At playtime the teasing began.

"Sylvester! Sylvester! What sort of a cissy name is that? Have you got on your vest? Sylvie, Sylvia, who's a pretty girl then?"

He began to cry and ran to hide beside the pegs in the cloakroom.

Wattie was home for a brief spell not long after. He listened to his son's tale of woe and laughed out loud.

"You can blame your mother for that stupid name." He glared at Mairead who was clearing the supper dishes. Sylvester noticed there were several black and blue marks on her bare arms.

"For pity's sake boy, you must be a good bit taller and heavier than some of these island brats. Why don't you stand up for yourself? Punch their noses, kick 'em where it hurts, whatever it takes. Stop being such a mammy's boy. Remember you're a Fin…" he hiccupped, "a Finlayson. I wasn't called Finn the Fist for nothing. Have a swallow of this; it'll make a man of you."

He belched loudly and passed the remains of his glass of beer to the boy. Sylvester drank it obediently trying not to choke on the strange taste. From now on he would be Finn Finlayson. Anyone who called him Sylvester would soon regret it.

Much later in life he was to acquire another nickname 'The Bradan' – the salmon – an elusive and slippery fish. With his sidekicks Roddy Cameron and the younger impressionable Neil Murray, Finn found himself on the wrong side of the law on many occasions. From harmless pranks such as leaving the local ladykiller's dilapidated bicycle overnight outside the house of a reclusive good-living spinster of the parish they progressed to deeds of increasing nastiness.

Finn was not the sort of boy to be content with pulling the wings off flies. Other larger equally harmless creatures fell foul of his vindictive nature. And there was other stuff. Petrol would go missing from Frasers' garage. A motorbike would race noisily over the moor road. A stolen mini-digger was found abandoned at the foot of the Arrochar rocks. Always the Bradan wriggled free of any blame. He had never left the house that night, just ask his mother.

Poor simple Shonnie Mackerichen's life was made a misery by their taunts and threats. As for the girls, Finn bragged that he could have his pick of any one but so far only the easy-going Bella Nandag had willingly obliged and paid the price with baby Whitney smiling from the big old pram.

Finn came home early one day to find his mother crying. An open envelope lay on the table and she was turning over some official looking type-written pages.

"What is it this time?" He scowled at her. "Father forgotten to put your money in the bank again?"

"No, not that, though we'll be lucky to see any more. This letter is from a firm of solicitors in Aberdeen. Seems your father was married already, he has a wife and family over there. That's why nobody on his side came to our wedding. That's why he was away from us so long." She dabbed her eyes with a crumpled tissue.

"I hope he never shows his face round here again!" roared Finn. "I'll give him Finn the Fist." He stamped out of the house in a red fury of rage. Cam and Neilly were coming up the track to meet him. They had plans for a carry-out before the dance that night in the hall. MacSweens' stores was to be the target if the old man could be distracted. Finn's news brought chortles of mirth from his mates. Neil laughed the loudest.

"You know what that makes YOU," he said derisively. Finn took a swipe at his head.

"Don't think for a minute that I give a damn. We're going to this dance to have a go at the girls. You know the one I'm after? Well boys, tonight's the night."

Recent tenants of the late Calum Gillies's croft had come up from Wiltshire, full of good intentions. The daughter, Jean-Ann, was a quiet little lass with a shy smile and glossy black hair. Finn had declared he'd be the first to get at her.

"In your dreams!" said Cam and Neilly. "She's way out of your league man."

The hall was packed. Local musicians kept up the pace as the dancers hooched and reeled and swung. Everyone was in the best of

18

form except Finn who had asked Jean-Ann for a dance and felt insulted by her gentle refusal. She was waiting for someone, she said. Later he noticed her dancing with the daftie, Shonnie, his innocent face beaming, his clumsy feet doing their best to keep up. Finn was incensed. He swaggered outside for another swig at his half bottle which to his annoyance he had been obliged to pay for. It was pitch black, the curtained windows of the hall let out little light. The Fear an Taighe called thanks to the band as one dance ended and invited dancers to take their partners for a Strip the Willow. This announcement was received with much enthusiasm and the noise level rose audibly.

Someone slipped cautiously out the side door. It was Jean-Ann, Finn couldn't believe his luck. Maybe the one she was waiting for hadn't turned up and she was out for a look. Finn was on her like a shot, grabbing her from behind and covering her mouth with his hand. She struggled and kicked as he dragged her behind the gorse bushes. Finn felt her silent scream under his sweaty open palm. He fumbled roughly with her clothing and almost spent himself with the thrill before thrusting into her. She lay limp beneath him as he pulled out.

His lust satisfied, Finn felt like shouting aloud as he swaggered off into the night. There would be questions asked but no blame could be laid on him. Hadn't everyone seen for themselves that the girl had been dancing with Shonnie Gòrach, the village idiot, who could easily have lost control of what little sense he possessed?

He took the short cut home behind the clipping sheds. It would be easy to persuade his devoted mother to lie about the time he came through the door.

"Sod off, Shonnie Gòrach," growled the Bradan. "We don't want you hanging about with us."

"But I've got the whisky. Look. Look!" Shonnie cried eagerly, holding up a half bottle of brown liquid. There was no label on it.

"That's sheep's pish! Yon's never whisky," said Neilly scathingly. "I wouldn't touch the stuff. It'll put you clean off your head."

Cam poked Shonnie's head with a nicotine-stained finger. "Is that what happened to you then?" he mocked. "Did you drink the sheep's pish or was it the paint stripper?"

"Leave me alone." Shonnie took a step back, clutching his bottle. He staggered and almost fell. His tormentors laughed.

"See what I mean!" hooted Neilly. "The damage has already been done. Bloody daftie, away home to your mammy."

Shonnie shuffled away, not looking back. He shoved the bottle into the wide top pocket of his dungarees, hitching them up again with the long length of rope he used for a belt. It did not bother him that a half-mast gap was left between trouser and boot. He rubbed his head angrily where Cam had jabbed him, the wispy brown hair already receding.

"The boys won't let me go to the rocks with them," he wailed, coming in the kitchen door. There was a fine smell. His mother was taking scones out of the oven, her face red from the heat.

"Is that Neilly and Cam at you again?" You'd best keep away from them. Seo, a' ghràidh, here's a nice hot scone. I'll put butter on it for you."

"The Bradan was there too. They wouldn't take a dram from my bottle."

Shonnie had the scone done in two bites. "Have you another one for me?" he rubbed his mouth with the back of a grimy hand.

Old Mrs Mackerichen sighed. Her poor laddie couldn't help himself. A late and unexpected addition to the family, he had always been different, difficult, misunderstood. Shonnie's daddy, astounded and proud at becoming a father again at 67, had fallen to his death some five years later at Creag nan Roin while searching for a lost sheep. Jumped off more likely, said some unkind tongues when it was seen that there was something the matter with little Shonnie, so

20

slow and unnatural and for a long time not a word of speaking in him.

Feeling it was her Christian duty Miss Mason at the wee school allowed him to attend in the afternoons. He concentrated very hard, licking his blunt pencil and rubbing out mistakes with a wet finger until the page was full of holes. Coloured crayons were much easier for him, he could draw a good picture and he loved the singing lessons. Miss Mason gave him the bell to ring when playtime was over. People looked out for him, and his widowed mother was helped in the kindly ways of island folk. Shonnie knew the names of wild flowers and recognised the songs of birds. He could tell each crofter's sheep by their keel marks and was a great help at the fank or the peats. When he grew older Shonnie learned to dance; he loved the ceilidh music and could blow a tune on an old harmonica brought home by a brother in the Merchant Navy.

"Watch out for the Bradan," warned Shonnie's mother. "He's the worst of the lot of them. Remember what happened to your cat."

No matter how often he was reported for wild driving or drunkenness somehow that scoundrel always wriggled free of blame, as elusive as the fish from which he got his name. There was the spit of him in the pram Bella Nandag paraded round the place.

"Are you minding there's a dance in the hall this Friday?" Shonnie's old mother was glad there was something for the laddie to take part in, a simple pleasure in his confined life. "Rory and Alec-Dan will be going, they'll take you along."

Shonnie's face broke into a smile. Some of his teeth were missing.

"I'll be able to dance with Morag and Kate and Jean-Ann won't I? Jean-Ann is bonnie, isn't she Mammy?"

"Right enough, she is that." His mother was washing up the bowls and spoons she'd just used. "I don't think she knows all that many folk yet, her people only took on Calum Gillies's croft last September".

By eleven on the night the hall was packed. Two button boxes and a fiddle belted out the familiar tunes. Murdani's drums kept them in time. The Highland Schottische, the Eightsome, Strip the Willow, everyone said it was one of the best nights there had been for ages. Daylight was coming in by the time the stragglers left for home.

Next day the place was in an uproar. The news was shocking and unbelievable. The wee lassie Jean-Ann with her raven hair and her shy smile had been the victim of an outrageous assault not far from the dance hall. A man with whisky on his breath had put her to the ground and forced himself on her. She had tried to call out … his hand was on her mouth. No, she did not recognise her attacker, she wept to the young policewoman who came out from the town. There were of course no witnesses.

Shonnie was with Bingo, his half- blind black collie the day the boys met him on the moor road. The Bradan, Cam and Neilly were aimlessly kicking a cork float back and fore. Shonnie came up to them with a hopeful smile.

"Can I get a game boys? I like a kick-about."

The Bradan stood squarely in front of him. "It's youself that should get more than a kick. Hurting the poor lassie like that."

"You're nothing but a bloody animal," taunted Cam. He aimed a spit at Shonnie's innocent face.

"I don't know what you're on about!" Shonnie's voice came out in a squeak.

"You did it with Jean-Ann didn't you? Well, say something. What was it like? Did she struggle?" Neilly's worked-up face leered at the terrified Shonnie.

"I had a dance with her, that was all, I swear to God. I wouldn't hurt a wee girl."

"You did, you did. We know it was you." The Bradan was enjoying this. "Willie Broad saw you, he said you were sweating after it."

Shonnie backed off in terror. He put his arms up over his head waiting for the blows he knew would come. The bigger boys thumped him and pushed him and shouted all manner of vile things. He had no idea what they meant.

"Stop it, stop it, let me be. I never did a thing," he yelled

Bingo bared his teeth in a snarl. The Bradan threw such a kick at his ribs that the poor dog let out a yelp and made off. Shonnie stumbled after him, crying now. He'd peed himself with the fear. He wanted only to get away from these terrible lies to a place where nobody would see him.

It was not that far to the moor, a bleak and lonely stretch, all heather and ancient peat cuttings. Many another lost sheep had strayed there, bleating forlornly in the wind which shrieked inland from the open sea. In the midst of this cheerless expanse one solitary tree still grew, moss-covered boulders round its foot, its twisted old limbs waving defiantly. A haunted place, said the storytellers reminiscing in the glow of a dying peat fire.

Shonnie clambered onto one of the cracked grey rocks. His legs wobbled weakly and a sound like angry buzzing bees dizzied his head as he untied his rope belt. Beneath the frowning clouds he made fast one end to a branch of the grim sentinel of the moor, the curlew's cry unheard as he looped the other carefully round his bending neck.

The Mind Boggles

'Maybe I should have gone up to town,' thought Johan as she opened the shop door. Once the MacSween sisters got hold of a piece of news they were better than any bush telegraph and everyone would know by tea time. As the bell pinged and wobbled above her head she smiled and stepped politely aside to let a tall lady pass. She was clutching a handful of postcards and said good morning very breezily. Johan said, "Yes, isn't it," as she negotiated the step.

There were no other customers. Peigi was rearranging magazines on a rack, inserting current ones and setting aside those out of date for return to the wholesalers. Dollag, senior by four years, was in her usual position behind the counter ostensibly tidying the assortment of items placed near the till to encourage last-minute summer spending – chewing gum, child-sized plastic sunglasses, lip balms, Scotland fridge magnets shaped like sheep, pocket packs of paper tissues and the remainder of the Cadbury's eggs from Easter, most of them with their foil packaging still intact.

"Good morning, Mrs Fraser." Dollag carefully removed one of the less well-wrapped eggs from the box; it would not do to let people think she was selling shoddy goods.

Johan picked up a packet of cornflakes, HP sauce, a Press and Journal and the last carton of duck eggs. There was just room on the counter for the wire basket.

"Would you like this chocolate egg for your wee Alan – it's got just a little bit torn?" Dollag enquired, moving the basket closer to her side of the counter.

"That's very kind, Dolina," replied Johan. "Oh and I'm wanting a bag of kindlers, I saw them round the side of the shop when I came in. Are they fine and dry?"

"Of course they are." Dollag began ringing the items carefully through the till, a contraption she was happy to have mastered. In her semi-retired father's day all calculations had been done with a well-licked pencil stub on the back of a paper bag. She told Johan the price.

"Will there be anything else?"

Johan cleared her throat, it was now or never.

"Can I have a look through your patterns? I'm away to do a bit of knitting."

Peigi obliged by bringing the thick selection-book to the counter.

"Was it something for Norrie, or yourself perhaps? There's nice Fair Isle ones here. Cathy Macaskill did a grand one for Don-Alec, last Christmas it would have been."

"No Peigi, it's the baby clothes I'm after, wee jackets, bootees, that sort of thing."

Johan was aware of the curious looks. Dollag's mouth hung open.

"You're not … are you, yourself?"

Johan felt her face colour.

"Well what if I am!" she laughed "It did come as a bit of a surprise, Norrie and me thought we were well past all that with four of a family already so it's taken a while to get used to the idea. Give me those two for matinee jackets and this one with the bonnets and mittens. Now, let's have a look at your wool – better make it lemon or white."

After the purchases had been wrapped and stowed in her shopping bag Johan turned to leave.

Dollag called out, "I'll send Neilly Murray round with your sticks in the barrow; you're not to go lifting them yourself."

"That would be a great help Dolina. Thanks a lot."

Johan closed the door gently, wishing she could be a fly on the wall once the sisters got her out of the way.

"What do you think of that?" was Dollag's opening remark. "Would you ever have guessed?"

"Never on earth," Peigi replied. "She's as stout anyway, you'd not know the difference. No wonder nobody noticed. Imagine, her and Norrie at their age? She must be well past forty. Och mo chreach! The mind boggles."

"What did you say?" Dollag asked crossly. "Boggles! what sort of word is that? You didn't pick that up from Radio nan Gaidheal."

"I said, 'the mind boggles'. It means you find it difficult to believe that something could actually be happening."

Peigi was pleased with her modern vocabulary.

Dollag was still somewhat offended.

"You'd think Sadie Graham might have said something; she's in here often enough. I never saw anyone buy so much talcum powder. You know she fancies Donnie Diesel on the bus."

Peigi was more realistic.

25

"But the District Nurse would have to be like the doctor himself, oaths of confidentiality and all that. And if her brother had got to know HE'D not have kept it to himself, there would have been more than the letters getting delivered to folk's doors."

The bell clattered again and Chrisanne Macintyre came in looking quite summery, her bright red dress and bare feet in matching sandals earning a look of disapproval from Dollag who nonetheless enquired solicitously about her and her husband's health and remarked on the fineness of the weather. With a cheerful cheerio Chrisanne left the shop carrying her sliced brown loaf. The sisters exchanged looks.

"I could tell you were dying to say something about Johan Fraser." Peigi tied up the last bundle of magazines and snipped the string economically. "It's not like you to miss a chance."

"What do you take me for, some village gossip?" Dollag glared. "We all know how much herself and the minister have looked forward to a family; it would have been unkind to broadcast Johan's fertility at the poor woman."

"Well, I never thought you were so sensitive," Peigi feigned surprise.

Dollag dusted off her hands. "Go you through and put the kettle on, Peigi. I see Aggie Bell the school cleaner and two of her cronies making for here. I'm sure they would be the better of a wee cup of tea."

Meeting Miss Mason

"But Granny, I don't really want to go to school." Beathag pleaded. "Can I not just stay here with you and the cats? I'll be good I promise. I'll feed the hens. I'll take in some peat for you."

Granny Morag wiped down the side of the sink and untied her apron.

"You're always good and you're always a help to me pet, it's not that I don't want you at home. It is the rules that you must go to school after you are five. Your daddy would get into trouble if he didn't put you there. Here he is coming now; I heard Bob barking. We'll just zip up your jacket; isn't that the pink colour you like best? Don't cry now. You will be fine once you're with the other boys and girls, and Miss Mason is a good teacher; she's been here a long time."

Well over six feet tall, Jacob MacDonald ducked his head as he came through the door. He picked Beathag up in his arms and whirled her round. She cried out for him to stop.

"You're making me dizzy, Daddy. Put me down."

It was the aeroplane game they had played since she was small, since before they had lost her Mammy. Jacob recalled only too well how his wife had courageously fought the impossible battle with leukaemia, growing smaller and more frail as they watched helplessly. Beathag was not quite three at the time and had only known the care of her Daddy's mother, her granny Morag, to whose house they had moved not long after Margaret Anne's final days at the Hospice. Jacob could not face the memories held within the building where they had set up home with such hopes for their future. It was now a holiday let and every summer new strangers appeared to fill its rooms with laughter again.

Morag's house was less than half a mile from the school and the shop and the church. Reluctantly Beathag set off, clasping her dad's hand for reassurance and trying to match her short steps to his long-legged stride. He thought how proud his wife would have been seeing their little girl starting her first day at school. After their loss he and his mother had tended to live a secluded life, consumed with anxiety lest something should happen to the child and Beathag seldom saw or mixed with the other village children.

Today was a big step for a shy little girl. Beathag pulled up the hood of her jacket even though the August morning was already showing promise of warmth to come. If she did not see too much perhaps it would not really be there. Bob was not allowed to come with them; Dad said Granny needed the dog to keep her company. Jacob had put on his tweed waistcoat and flat cap instead of the rough working jacket and woolly tammy he normally wore. The sturdy stone dykes sheltered them from the worst of the chill wind from across the bay. Beathag said it felt like the sea was moving inside her tummy. Dad told her that people often felt like that when they were going to do something they'd not done before. It would all be grand and he'd come for her at dinner time.

Many of the village folk depended on Jacob for ploughing and harvesting and bringing trailer loads of peats home from the moor. Nothing was too much trouble for him. He was a skilful shepherd and had a way with all animals in sickness. Some said he was as good as the vet who came reluctantly and expensively from town.

The playground was noisy with youngsters running around. Miss Alice Mason appeared at the school door. She wore a dark green two piece suit with a cameo brooch pinned to the collar of a pale lemon blouse. A shrill blast on the whistle made Beathag jump. Immediately two lines formed, boys and girls, and the pupils walked quietly indoors. Everyone except Beathag and one wee boy seemed to know what to do next. Miss Mason spoke briefly to Jacob and Mrs Fraser who had brought her youngest son.

"Leave them with me," she said curtly. "It's always best if the parents go right away. You can collect them at mid-day. Good Morning."

She closed the door.

Beathag MacDonald and Alan Fraser followed the teacher obediently into the big room which held all of the sixteen pupils including Alan's older brother and sister, twins Duggie and Evie. The two new entrants sat next to each other at one of the smaller desks while Miss Mason opened the register and began to read out names.

"Here Miss," each nominee answered in turn.

"Elizabeth Anne MacDonald."

No reply. The name was repeated more loudly. Still silence. Miss Mason looked down over her half-moon glasses.

28

"Answer when your name is called," she said sharply. "You are Elizabeth Anne MacDonald are you not?"

"No," a shaky little voice replied. "I'm Beathag MacDonald."

Miss Mason closed the thin blue book with a snap.

"In this class you will answer to Elizabeth Anne. All eyes closed for the Lord's Prayer."

The children repeated the ancient words. Instructions to the older ones followed. Miss Mason handed the newcomers a page of plain paper and a small box of crayons and told them to draw a picture of their mammy and daddy. Beathag's anxious face turned to the teacher.

"I can't," she whispered, putting the lid back on the crayon box.

"And why can't you may I ask?" Miss Mason did not like to be crossed.

Roddy William MacLennan spoke respectfully from the back of the class where the older ones sat.

"Please Miss, her mother died a while ago when she was only wee. She has her granny though," he added encouragingly.

How could she have forgotten that! Alice Mason chided herself silently. Time for retirement had long since come and gone. She clung to her work as a means of survival, putting off the moment when she would have to face a cheerless future in her home town of Falkirk. There, her own aged mother, acid-tongued and wandering in her mind, was being cared for in an expensive respite home.

The two little artists in the front seats worked away. Miss Mason was surprised by the quality of the picture produced by the shy child.

"Tell me about your picture," she said, not unkindly. Beathag pointed carefully at the figures standing on the spiky grass.

"That's Daddy, that's me, that's Granny with her Sunday hat on. Here's Bob the collie and Flora and Fergus our cats." There were lots of bushy white clouds and what looked like someone asleep on top of them. A bearded figure loomed above.

"And that's my mammy with Father Wishart. Our Father Wishart in Heaven," she added solemnly.

Miss Mason played the piano for singing. Beathag liked the song about some little ducks until the last bit where none of the ducks came back. After playtime wooden bricks and some small toys were set out for the very youngest while the older classes worked at maths exercises or read aloud in turn. Beathag needed to go to the bathroom. She did not know where it might be. Perhaps she had to wait till she got home. It became clear that this was not an option. When a little damp puddle appeared on the plastic play-mat Beathag feared she was in big trouble. She began to cry, clutching her tartan skirt desperately in the hope of stemming the flow. Miss Mason summed up the situation promptly.

"These little accidents do happen," she told the sobbing child.

"Evelyn Fraser. Please take Elizabeth Anne to the toilets." From a drawer in her desk she discreetly produced a clean pair of pants. She wondered again at her lack of competence in overlooking the fact that the MacDonald girl had never attended any pre-school activities and thus would have no idea of the daily routines. She frowned. Her letter of resignation, long since drafted out, must surely be in the post without delay.

Beathag was overjoyed to see her father appear at twelve o'clock in his red Massey Ferguson tractor, a familiar sight in the village and beyond. She clambered happily up the muddy metal steps and squeezed into the cosy cab. It was a special day for Jacob as well as he seldom took time off work. He asked his daughter how she had got on and listened sympathetically as she told how awful it had been about her name being wrong and about wetting herself.

"Miss Mason says I have to bring back the spare pants after they've been washed. What will Granny say?"

Jacob thought angrily not about Granny's reaction but about the words he himself intended to say to the school teacher next day. He had heard stories of her strict attitude, her indifference to the island way of life, coming down hard on pupils who used Gaelic in the classroom. Villagers who tried to approach her had had their friendly overtures rejected.

Bob came running to meet the tractor, barking an eager welcome.

"I can't wait to see Granny!" Beathag exclaimed. "Daddy, do I have to go back there tomorrow?"

"It will be better tomorrow," her father replied. "I am going to have a wee chat with the teacher."

At the beginning of September word got about that Miss Mason was retiring after mid-term. Nobody was sorry, but when the time came round tradition insisted that they held a farewell gathering in the village hall. Surprisingly it turned out to be quite an occasion.

Her replacement was a young single English lady who longed to sample island life. The novelty of westerly gales and driving rain soon wore off and she scurried away to be replaced by a more mature woman from the quiet town of Kelso who, commendably, survived almost twice as long. An aunt of Roddy William's was then persuaded out of retirement and took up lodgings with his parents much to his embarrassment. He couldn't wait to move on to High School.

Always first with the news, Hector MacSween in the General Stores reported on April 24th that a new young teacher was taking over after the summer holidays. It was said she had Skye connections 'but she would be none the worse for that' he added confidentially to anyone who would listen.

Letting Go

The brown-tinged newspaper at the bottom of her trunk was dated 1958. Alice Mason looked again, had it been almost forty years since she had come to take sole charge of this small island school? She placed the first layer of bedding on top of the face of a youthful-looking Duke of Edinburgh solemnly presenting an award to some young chap. This was not how she had expected to end her career but it had become obvious that with her reluctance to adapt to more up to date teaching methods and because the age for retirement had long since come and gone it was indeed time to let go.

The shame of that day when she had totally overlooked the needs of a shy 'first day at school' infant and the well deserved reproach she had received from her quiet-spoken father had left her in no doubt that the drafted letter of resignation should be posted forthwith. And yet, with the time for departure looming, she felt considerable regret for the way things might have been had she not been so determinedly set in her ways. Neighbourly approaches by villagers, invitations to take part in local activities, she had ignored them all. She recalled with dismay the dismissive way she had rejected the well-intentioned offer from the English ladies one Christmas. Gifts from Harrods indeed!

In the early days the emphasis had been on the three R's, the children learning by heart their tables and spelling and verses from the Bible. In a continuing routine each day would begin with a hymn and a prayer and pupils did what they were told without question. Speaking Gaelic in class was strictly forbidden; Alice Mason considered it not worth encouragement.

"It will only hold you back if you want to get on in the world," was her opinion.

She disapproved strongly when pounds, shillings and pence were replaced by decimal money – no more neat rows to be added and subtracted, no more struggling to 'change £17. 15s and ninepence halfpenny to halfpences', the children chewing their pencils through each laborious step. Weighing and measuring brought further problems, children were encouraged to learn by experimenting with water and sand and other messy substances, such nonsense being tolerated thanks to the uncomplaining support of Aggie Bell, the school cleaner.

Then different methods for reading and arithmetic in structured programmes appeared at the insistence of the Education Authorities. A T.V. set was installed and concessions made toward programmes on Nature Study or Ways of life from Bygone Days. Anything involving the workings of the human body or embarrassing associations between male and female was totally taboo. Miss Mason reckoned there was no call for children to hear about such things.

The class did look forward to a BBC Radio programme called 'Singing Together' which was accompanied by a cheerfully illustrated booklet containing the words. The teacher still recalled the horror of seeing the entry in the daily news journal of a child from a staunch Free Church household which read, 'Today we start Sinning Together.'

She thought back to the many who had passed through her care; several had gone on to follow careers in medicine and teaching and the ministry; others had gone far from home.

"There's nothing on the island for you," she would point out. "If you want to make something of yourselves you will need to get away."

Some of those who preferred family ties and loyalties had managed well enough. Sadly one or two had gone off the rails altogether and more than one had died too young by accident or at their own hands.

Packman's Removers were due on Wednesday. There was no time to linger on what might have been. With utmost care she wrapped the tea-set which had been in the family a long time, clusters of mauve ivy leaves creeping over the white bone china, to be brought out only for important occasions. The delicate cups and saucers had seldom moved from their glass-fronted display – perhaps once or twice before the old minister retired. Social exchanges had not been her way of life; too much familiarity tended to lessen one's authority. She had never understood the simple customs of Highland hospitality and she regretted to say it was much too late now.

Rising to ease the stiffness in her knees Alice Mason turned to items of furniture beside which cardboard boxes waited to accommodate papers and documents gathered over the years. She had already ruthlessly consigned to the fire items now considered irrelevant. From the bureau's flat top she removed the only family photograph she possessed of her mother and father, sternly posed, with herself and sister Geraldine unsmiling in front. Frivolity was frowned on in their strict household; fraternisation with young people outside the restrictive boundaries of the Church was not to be tolerated. The Mason sisters had been seen as old maids of the Parish even when they were young.

Father had passed away some years back and her mother, now senile and cantankerous, was in very costly residential care. Alice wondered how she would afford to continue these arrangements on a pension. It had been one of the reasons for retaining her teaching post for as long as she had. Geraldine was helping of course, giving private piano tuition from the gloomy family home to which she had returned after the stroke which had limited their father's speech and mobility. Mother had even then begun to find life confusing but had stubbornly refused to allow strangers interfering in their private concerns.

Miss Mason glanced at the space on the wall where her clock had hung, drawing in her breath sharply as she remembered why it was no longer there. Her wristwatch told her it was past time for a break for tea and a bite to eat. From the kitchen she could hear the tortured squeaks of the playground swings which roused her annoyance. Who had dared to defy the prohibition? She stepped no further than the back door before recollecting that as from the previous Friday she no longer had any authority.

The official goodbyes had been said at a surprisingly well-attended farewell gathering in the Village Hall. Reverend MacIntyre and Hector MacSween from the shop had both held forth making, she thought, exaggerated references to the 'praiseworthy' work she had carried out over the years. Everyone wished her a long and happy retirement and she was invited to accept some small tokens of appreciation from the community. The oldest and youngest pupils then climbed the three steps to the stage and smilingly handed over an envelope which she later found contained a good sum of money and some book tokens. There was also a beautiful framed photograph of herself surrounded by all fifteen pupils plus the indomitable Aggie Bell. The local photographer had at the time referred to 'something for the archives.'

Having been advised in advance as to what had been planned Miss Alice Mason had prepared a brief speech which to everyone's

34

surprise concluded with the words, "Mòran taing a h-uile duine –
thank you all very much."

There was a deafening round of applause as the threadbare beige
curtains slowly closed.

The Right Move

'Island School to close if no Teacher found'. As the crowded bus jerked and roared aggressively through the morning traffic Shona Nicolson thought about the headline she had read during a brief glimpse of the weekly West Coast paper. She shifted her legs uncomfortably, balancing the bulging bag of corrected maths workbooks awkwardly on her knees. Why was it always some bloke reeking of stubbed-out cigarette and last night's beer who chose to sit next to her? She turned her head discreetly to the steamed-up window, just two more stops till the inner-city school where she taught.

Almost four years – she could hardly believe it. Thank heavens it was Friday. Most of the children were good, willing to learn and eager to co-operate but there was always one or two whose insolence and disruptive behaviour made her days difficult and cost her many a night of disturbed sleep. Discipline had become harder to achieve and since the last head-master had taken 'early retirement' a succession of interim substitutes had failed to make any significant difference.

'Island School to close...' Shona promised herself a serious look at the article as soon as she got home from work.

After a shared spag-bol her two flatmates Carly and Roz got their 'pulling' gear on and headed for Fazoo's 'Dance-till-Dawn' assuring her that they would come in quietly – if they came in at all. Attempts to coax Shona along to this buzzing night-spot met with polite refusal in spite of her on-off relationship with Greg Anderson being in a distinctly chilly phase. It would be better for her, he kept insisting, if she would move in with him away from the influence of the other two who he considered giddy and irresponsible. "No thanks," she told him. "I have a laugh with the girls. They never criticise how I speak or what I wear." Last week in a rather up-market restaurant Greg had proposed, dramatically going down on one knee. Shona felt nothing but embarrassment as other diners watched with curiosity no doubt expecting a joyous acceptance.

With the flat to herself, Shona studied in detail the account of the plight of the island village school whose pupils would face a lengthy twice-daily bus trip in all weathers if their little school was forced to shut down. Two supply teachers had hurried back to civilisation at the first onslaught of winter's gales and non-stop rain, and the elderly retired lady at present in charge had made it clear that she would not be able to continue beyond the end of June. The realities of island living which may have deterred some was not a concern for Shona, herself born and raised on the island of mist and mountains only a regular ferry journey away from the one with the threatened school.

Other than the convenience of shops and public transport there was nothing about city life which she would miss. She thought it over for several days and talked at length on the phone with her parents who encouragingly approved of the idea. When Shona came home for her Easter break they could discuss it further. If the authorities considered her suitable she could be ready to start when the new session began in August.

"Are you sure you have thought his through properly?" Carly, city born and bred, was aghast at the prospect of such deprivation.

Roz was equally dubious.

"You know there will be no decent shops, no nightlife and little chance of any 'talent' among the heather and the hills. You'll be bored silly in no time."

Following a successful interview and an Easter-break reconnoitre of the little village Shona had no hesitation before tendering her resignation and forming plans for her big move. The small adjacent schoolhouse still contained carpets and several items of furniture abandoned by a former tenant, a Miss Mason – nothing modern but serviceable and in good condition. Shona's parents insisted on providing other useful items including a comfortable bed, pans, dishes, cutlery – none of which she had needed in the rented city property. A gleaming new angle-poise reading lamp was their special 'housewarming' gift.

Greg Anderson's reaction had been predictable.

"I'll give you till Christmas," was his scornful comment and, no, he did not anticipate visiting. Shona tried hard to look disappointed.

She was aware of the stir a new arrival would create in a small place. Her parents and brother Sandy had helped her move in, installing a cooker and washing machine and repositioning heavier furniture. For this help she was grateful but it was nothing like the satisfaction she felt organising cupboards and wardrobes, finding places for books and CDs, putting up pictures – the heady anticipation of a new future in her own little domain.

There were three weeks till term began, time to get the classroom organised, check the equipment available and familiarise herself with names in the register to which she could soon put faces. The brief Easter visit had shown her where to find the village shop, the church and to her relief a garage. Her recently acquired Fiat Punto had a lot of miles on the clock and she was pleased to see there was still a petrol pump.

In the quiet of a summer evening Shona took her mug of coffee out to the small walled garden. Once some of the tangled bushes had been cut back, she reckoned, there was a lot could be done with it. Perhaps involve the children, get them interested in growing things. Much would depend on the weather. Rhubarb grew in abundance; she'd borrow her mother's jam pan and ask around for empty jars. Everyone she had met so far had been extremely welcoming, and offers of help had come from most unexpected sources including one elderly chap who introduced himself as the local shoemaker. He had arrived on an ancient bicycle and seemed in no hurry to leave. The ladies in the shop were pleasant if a trifle inquisitive, their elderly father being heavily involved in village matters. A cheerful wee woman called Aggie who was both cook and cleaner at the school seemed to know everything that was important about everybody in the area. Shona took to her right away. A youngish man on a dusty red tractor had brought some potatoes and two bags of peats 'just to get you started,' he'd said awkwardly, hurrying on his way.

All she needed now was a dog. There were stretches of hill and shore just asking to be explored. Shona sighed with pure contentment. She knew she had made the right move.

Wandering Joan

The fox was at the hens last night, I heard them gok-gawking. What could I have done about it, a man well past his three score and ten? By the time I'd have swung the old legs out of the bed and found my slippers and the gun the rascal would have been over the rigs and far beyond. I will ask Jimmy to look where it might be getting in.

The Lord has blessed me in so many ways. I have a good roof over my head and a pension of money that sees to my needs. And lucky I am too that a son and a daughter still live here with me though others have put distance between us in the need to find work. It has given me much happiness that just this week Kendra, my youngest, is here from south of the border. Her husband has been sent to Dubai to 'fulfil a contract.' Am I not good with these fine words? They'll be putting me on television next. Anyway, Kendra is here with the children for two weeks, then they are going ski-ing to some foreign place with a difficult name.

The boy Christopher is quiet and steady like his uncle Jimmy was in his young day. I would like to see him get out and about a bit more but he sits most of the time in the house with some noisy gadget that he works with great concentration and watches things jumping about on a little glass screen. Imogen, the sister, is quite the opposite, a tomboy you could call her even with that fancy name. She wants to be off on Sadie's old bike or climbing the hill or splashing about in the sea. We were all round the fire after supper when she told us she was going to the caves next day, she'd take the big torch and spend time exploring.

"You must be very careful there," I said solemnly to her. "Has nobody told you about Wandering Joan?"

"Who? Never heard of her." Imogen said quite smartly, but I could see she was curious. And Christopher switched off the sound of gunfire and turned to look my way. I took the cup of tea from Sadie's hand and rested my feet in their socks on that fat leather cushion thing, I can never remember the name they have for it.

"She was a girl from the village, a few years older than you are now, Imogen. Because she had one leg that was shorter than the other the children laughed at her with the big black boot. Her parents tried to keep her close to home as much as they could in case she would come to harm. But Joan was not happy with these restrictions

39

and she'd be off and away as soon as nobody was looking, even when darkness was coming down and you'd be surprised how fast she could shift herself for one so cripple.

"More than once they had people out searching and she would be in awful trouble when they got her home but that never stopped her, even when she was no longer a child. It seemed as if she was always searching for something beyond what she had." I took a sip of my tea.

"Early one morning, the story goes, she set off for the shore just like you are planning for tomorrow. It was in the Brown Seals' cave, farther than she had ever gone, that she found the circle of white stones. Hoping for the power they might possess she stepped inside and shut fast her eyes for a wish. At once her feet were sucked down into the sand and the creeping dark of the cave closed in around her. From somewhere she could hear a mewling cry like a kitten might make and being soft-hearted she wanted to go and look for it.

"But try as she might her feet remained stuck fast. She became aware that the pillar of rock in front of her was not rock at all but a young man straight and tall like the mast of a boat, his eyes as dark as midnight pools. His strong hands lifted her without effort.

"'You are here and the time of waiting is over,' he said. 'It is right that we will be together.'

"He led her up a flight of stony steps and into open air where the sun beamed down from a wide clear blue sky. To Joan's great joy the ugly boot had vanished, just as she had wished, and her feet trod lightly.

"'This is Daonnan, the land of Always,' he said proudly. 'You will be safe with me, Strong Niall of the Well. Here you will hear no voices raised in anger, no illness will bring you down, no child will cry in the night, no sudden squalls of wet will sweep down from the hills. Youth and beauty will ever be yours in this place but you must not at any time seek the Steps of Return. Now, this very night, the seeds of love will be sown.'

"Many weeks and months and years went by. Their family numbered five, their crops flourished, their cows bore healthy calves every spring. Joan had never dreamed of such perfect happiness and memories of an earlier life did not come to trouble her contentment.

"Then came the day when she heard again the pitiful mewing of a kitten crying helplessly, an unexpected sound in this enchanted place. Without a second thought Joan laid down her basket of mushrooms and set off to follow the plaintive sound. On and on she walked, all else forgotten, not noticing that the path grew narrow and the sky darkened overhead.

"She found herself at the top of the stone steps. The mewling of the creature could be faintly heard from somewhere down below. Ignoring the warning that she must never seek the Steps of Return Joan let her feet carry her further and further away from Daonnan, sure in the knowledge that she would find her way back."

I swallowed the last of my tea and put the empty cup on the table. No-one spoke.

"But this was not to be. She felt the smell of the sea as she plunged forward through the mouth of the cave where her wondrous journey had begun. To her utmost dismay the hand she raised to smooth back her tangled hair was old and wrinkled. Her tongue could feel the gaps in her mouth where not long before had been sound strong teeth. And worst of all, her foot was once again dragged down by the clumsy black boot.

"She hobbled on and on, finally reaching the place which she recognised as home. At the front door she paused, anxious of the scolding she would surely receive. Her mother, bent and haggard, came at her knocking but showed no signs of recognition even as Joan ventured to explain all that had befallen her. It was a year and a day since their daughter went missing, she was told. They still prayed each waking hour for her safe return.

"'But because you are old and surely have come far we will offer you a bite to eat and a resting place till the new day,' the mother went on.

"And so it happened, Joan passed the night asleep in the room of her childhood while her parents tiptoed through the house fearful of disturbing their aged guest.

"In the morning Joan's mother tapped discreetly on the bedroom door and opened it gently to offer refreshment to the old woman. She looked all around but could see nothing save for a strange grey cat curled up peacefully upon the quilt. Wandering Joan was never seen again."

The silence lasted only moments before Imogen spoke.

"Thanks, Grandfather, that was a great story but you know, I don't believe a word of it and it certainly won't put me off exploring the cave tomorrow. Don't worry; I will watch out for the white stones!" She giggled.

Imogen picked up an apple from the bowl on the dresser and nodded to her brother to follow her through to the room. They would sit there in front of the television and happily accept for real events every bit as unlikely as those they had just heard.

My daughters were laughing together. "Well I remember you telling us all that stuff when we were children," Sadie said. "I don't think the young folk today are so likely to take it to heart."

"It's not that," I told her. "It isn't so long till we will be coming into a new century with its changing ways and modern ideas and it would be a pity if the story-telling tradition was to die away. So much would be lost."

They said how much they agreed with me and how well they remembered this tale and the other. 'Black Duncan from Skye' had been a big favourite.

"That one can keep for another day." I left them to their washing up and went off out to see if Jimmy had the hens' place secured. If he hadn't, by Jove I would have something to say about it!

The Turn of the Century

Hector MacSween of the General Stores was renowned for his punctuality, anyone failing to live up to his stringent standards bore the brunt of his serious displeasure. In the dwindling light of an early November day a select group of members of the Community Hall Committee restlessly awaited MacSween's return from town. Watches were being consulted and suppositions voiced. After weeks of delay they had been told that the curtains for hanging in front of the Hall stage were ready for collection. The first set had proved somewhat inadequate – errors in measuring could not be ruled out and blame was quietly ascribed to more than one of the enthusiastic volunteers.

The rear reflectors of Hector's dark green Volvo showed up in the headlights of the bus as it covered the last stretch before the moor road turn-off. Driver Donnie Campbell scrambled down the bank to where the car lay at an awkward angle. Emergency services arrived promptly in response to his 999 call. There was nothing they could do. Dolina and Peigi took the news of their father stoically; they pulled down the blinds and closed the Stores. Suddenly the curtains became unimportant.

In the lead-up to the millennium restoration of the village hall had been the agreed-on major project. A Lottery grant had been negotiated to augment some intensive local fund-raising, and before they left at the end of August the two English ladies had made a generous donation by way of thanks for their acceptance into the community back in 1993.

Now the hall featured a gleaming new kitchen and a special fit-for purpose room where Nurse Sadie Graham could hold clinics. A more solid dance floor replaced the creaking boards which had sagged and bounced through many a reel and schottische. The stage had lighting and proper steps with a hand rail and the cloakroom facilities were given a much-needed up-grade which included disabled access. School cleaner Aggie Bell had in true Annika Rice fashion sought out, coaxed, cajoled and bullied the best of local tradesmen. The available funds were considerable and the standard of workmanship expected to be of the best – a plumber had come from as far away as Tolsta. Shifts of volunteers had helped in whatever way they could dispensing refreshment and encouragement and conflicting advice.

In common with towns and villages country-wide the inhabitants of this remote place had debated at length as to how the turn of the century should be marked. There would of course be a time-capsule, every family to be invited to have their details and photographs recorded for posterity. The level of co-operation exceeded all expectations, new bonnets for the bodachs and items of ladies' finery had been acquired and Rosie Bain from the town's 'Clip and Curl' had a waiting list for her services.

"Not what we need," said the local photographer and the man from the paper. "People in the future will want to see you as you are … swinging a scythe, milking a cow, tying up a boat … not looking like models from a catalogue who couldn't tell a tup from a camel in the zoo."

The unstoppable Aggie had also come up with the idea of a wall-hanging. This would be a plain piece of linen cloth upon which each person could sign their name in biro pen. Cara Bingham from the craft shop volunteered to take on the task of embroidering over each one in coloured threads. Expecting her third in the Spring she welcomed the opportunity of a restful contribution. With no children of her own and her husband often away on pastoral duties Chrisanne from the Manse willingly accompanied Aggie as her little grey van criss-crossed the countryside until all the signatures had been collected.

As 1999 slowly wound to a close, levels of excitement rose rapidly especially in the school where rehearsals for a pageant of the century had almost taken over from normal routines. Miss Nicolson's natural concerns proved unfounded as it was, as they say 'all right on the night.' In a scene representing the Great War nine year old Alan Fraser proudly displayed a row of his grandfather's medals. A small group of relatives waved a tearful farewell as the Metagama sounded its siren before sailing with emigrants to America. Quiet Beathag MacDonald posed regally as Her Majesty on her Coronation Day, another pupil made a splendid moon landing wearing a motorbike helmet covered with bubble-wrap and lifting his feet with difficulty in his Dad's heavy boots. Former pupil Roddy William stole the show with his Elvis impersonation, cavorting madly to the sound

44

track of 'Hound Dog'. As the smart green curtains finally closed the applause shook the roof.

The final minutes of 1999 were counted down in a high state of anticipation and as the bells rang out on the new sound system an enormous cheer arose and every glass was raised to toast the new century. Even normally reserved folk exchanged hugs and good wishes before forming a circle to sing 'Auld Lang Syne'. Then the Reverend MacIntyre called for quiet in order to lead the company in prayer before the frail figure of ninety five year old Minnie Fraser, mother of Norrie from the garage, was led out from the side of the stage. Having seen more New Years than anyone else in the place it seemed appropriate that she should perform the task of pulling a cord which drew back two red velvet curtains to reveal a small wooden plaque.'

"In respectful memory of Hector Morrison MacSween, a stalwart supporter of this Millennium Project." The old lady read out the words in an unexpectedly firm voice. There were gasps of surprise and approval. This had been a very well-kept secret.

Kenny Grant blew up his pipes and led the company outdoors to where fireworks were already dazzling the night sky and the lights of two beacons could be seen across the glen.

It was a time to reflect and remember, to look forward in the precious hope of peace and continuity and in curious speculation as to what the new century might bring.

Mothers and Daughters

"We're a right pair yourself and myself Bob." Granny Morag stroked the collie's wise old head. She closed the shed door and turned back to the house.

"It must be old age coming over me – when I looked in that shed I had no idea what I came out for. And last week when the Minister called about some wedding detail didn't I pour him a cup of hot water! Where were the teabags? Still in the tin. He just laughed about it and said things like that happened to him all the time and, well, he's a good few years younger than me!"

Bob flopped down on the rug in front of the Rayburn and rested his head between his paws. Morag poured water into his drinking bowl.

"And are you remembering yourself what it was like running up the hill for the sheep when your legs were young and strong? Mirk might have taken over your job but there will always be a place for you here. Beathag and I would be lost without you."

'And will there be a place for me?' the old lady pondered. What would happen when her son Jacob got married again? Morag was glad for him; it was more than ten years since Beathag's mother's death. It had taken him long enough to think himself a suitable match for the nice young schoolteacher. So bashful, and never too good with words, it was just as well that Miss Nicolson, Shona, had given him some gentle encouragement. His mother knew for a fact that there had been more than one overnight stay but Jacob was always home before Beathag got up, responding awkwardly to his mother's delicate questioning, his face the colour of the blossom on the rose.

Morag got on well with Shona but there was a niggling worry they would want their own place – two women sharing a kitchen was never a good idea. She would speak to Jacob soon. The wedding in Rev. MacIntyre's church was to be at the start of the Easter holidays with the refurbished Village Hall already booked for the celebrations to follow.

The bitter February weather showed no sign of letting up. Jackets and mittens dried slowly on classroom radiators and Miss Nicolson and Aggie, her dinner lady, had taken it upon themselves to make sure every pupil had a mug of hot cocoa at morning playtime. It was ten year old Beathag MacDonald's turn to be 'mug monitor', capably carrying the tray of empties through to Aggie's sink. No longer the timid child who had encountered the awful Miss Mason on her first day of school, Beathag had gained in confidence and shone at her lessons. Her drawings adorned the classroom walls and the kitchen at home and she greatly enjoyed her involvement in the end of term concerts. Her most important role yet would be at her father's marriage to the teacher – she was to be a junior bridesmaid along with one of Shona's pals from her Glasgow days.

'Shona – Miss Nicolson – Mam even?' Beathag was more than a little concerned as to what name she would be expected to use. Her Granny told her she would still say 'Please Miss' in the classroom, nobody ever said 'Please Mrs.' Beathag recalled how difficult it had been at first with the two English ladies who had been so kind to her, she never felt quite right calling them Lavinia and Beryl even though they insisted.

Their wee pony Flossie had been a parting gift to Beathag. It was not possible to take her to Edinburgh they explained. They needed someone who would look after her properly. Lavinia had discovered a wonderful old bookshop for sale in a street just off the Royal Mile. The decision to move had not been taken lightly as many friends had been made since their arrival in 1993 which had aroused such curiosity. They bought a flat in Moray Place, a much sought after part of the city, and Beathag was to come and visit when she was a bit older. And yes, Dad had said, they would be coming to the wedding.

Shona Nicolson carried her after-lunch coffee through to the little staff room. Mishaps in the playground were thankfully few but she liked to be reachable if anyone needed her. No final decision had been made as to where they would live after they were married. Shona intended to call on Jacob's mother again to make sure she would be happy for them to come to her. Jacob's own house had become a holiday let soon after his first wife's death. It had held too many sad memories for him. The schoolhouse was more than adequate but should the need at some future date arise for a supply teacher then accommodation would be a sensible and encouraging option.

Re-reading that morning's letter from her own mother Shona felt almost embarrassed by the enthusiastic and glowing appreciation of her fiancé. The Nicolsons were delighted that their daughter had found someone so special – 'not like that pompous drip you had in tow in Glasgow.' That one-off meeting with her parents had not been a success.

'Now,' the letter continued, 'About the Procession'. Shona groaned. Her father wanted to observe the old highland tradition of the bridal party and guests being led from the bride's house by a piper to where the reception would be held.

"Even in good weather it would be rather far," Shona had protested, mindful as well of the footwear of the day. The compromise, it seemed, had been acceptable to the Nicolson household and on the day, weather allowing, they would 'process' only from the church to the road end where cars and a hired bus would be waiting.

In an excited Email Shona's bridesmaid Carly, a flatmate from Glasgow days, had begged for details of the best man.

'Sorry,' Shona had replied. 'All I can tell you is that his name is Seoras – that's George in Gaelic. He once worked over at Home Farm but he's on the rigs now. Jacob reckons you'll get on fine. He has plenty to say for himself. You'll just have to wait till the big day!'

She pressed the electric bell signalling the end of breaktime.

In the cosy kitchen Morag had her son's dinner keeping warm in the oven. The frosty weather was grand for ploughing and he was late back from the long field.

"Have you everything ready for school tomorrow? Away off to bed a'ghráidh, I'll come up in a while and put off your light."

"Night night Granny," Beathag gave the old lady a hug.

"Good night Miss Nicolson."

"Good night Beathag, see you tomorrow." Shona longed to reach out her arms to the child. It was too soon.

"Beathag was asking me…" Morag began awkwardly, "what would she call you after you and her Dad are married."

"I'd be happy with 'Shona' outside of school. I know it must be difficult for her, I'm not her Mammy but who knows, some day if we get her a baby brother or sister . . ." She left the sentence unfinished.

48

"And Morag," she went on. "If it's fine with you we thought it best if we all lived here. It's been home to all three of you and I'd be really happy to share it. But remember we would not expect everything done for us. Admittedly I'd need you to keep me right with the cooking – you know what Jacob likes. There's lots of things we could manage between us but I'd want you to do the oatcakes; nobody does them better."

"Och lassie it's just plain things. You'll do grand I am quite sure …and I have to tell you it's a huge relief to know you will all be here. I didn't want to be left on my own."

Shona stood up. "Oh Morag, there was never any chance of that being an option. Come here." She put her arms round the old woman's shoulders. "You are very dear to us all."

The dogs stirred at the sound of the back door closing. Jacob came through pulling off his woollen tammy, his face rosy with the cold, his eyes lighting up with the warmest smile.

"My two favourite ladies," he said, walking towards them in his stockinged feet.

Pushing the Boat Out

"Why do I always have to go to Auntie Mina's for the holidays? I'm sixteen now – I could be away with my pals somewhere nice. It's so boring over there and she makes me do all the work like some unpaid skivvy." I didn't think for a minute that my mother would listen.

"Come on Jessica, you know poor Mina's on her own since Uncle Willie died. She just wants a bit of company and she is your father's oldest sister."

There would be no arguing. My cousin Flag fetched me in the car as usual. The tiny middle room at the top of the stairs hadn't changed a bit over the years. There was a strict rule against pinning stuff up on the walls. One single framed photo of a be-whiskered long-dead relative frowned down on me. When I was much younger I thought it was God. It put me on my best behaviour I can tell you.

As soon as I was back downstairs Mina had me off looking for eggs. There was a bantam laying away.

"I'll give you a cup of tea when you get back."

I groaned, knowing how stewed it would be. There's never coffee, it keeps her awake. No Cola, no Irn-Bru. If the rain went off I might be sent for messages and I'd get some at the shop. Only last year the MacSween sisters had installed a bigger chill cabinet.

The days dragged wearily by until the Tuesday when Jimmy the Post brought the airmail letter. What a commotion that set up! Mina came through to the scullery where I was finishing the breakfast dishes.

"Look at this!" She waved the missive triumphantly. "Willie-Douglas and his wife are coming over for a visit. They'll be here on Saturday. We'd better get going, there's so much we need to do."

'We'…I thought resignedly. This would mean a total blitz on every square inch of the place and guess who'd be doing the donkey work? Ever since my cousin Willie-Douglas had taken up residence in America Auntie Mina had sung his praises and boasted of his accomplishments to anyone who would show the slightest interest. It was 'my son this, my son that'. For goodness sake, when he left here he was a garage mechanic. Now it seemed he was running the entire motor industry of Detroit City. I was told to take down the curtains in the back bedroom, WD's old room. Mina was on the phone for ages;

so many people had to be informed of the prodigal's return. She started making lists. I got the steps out from below the stairs.

Flag was summoned the following day and we headed for the town with the lists. My mother was meeting us after the dentist's; she'd cracked a tooth on a ginger snap. Flag and myself carried the stuff. Sheets and pillowcases, white tablecloths, a new set of dishes, these perfumey things you plug into a socket – even some tumblers that were supposed to look like crystal. In the Co-op the ladies did the grocery/bakery bit and Flag was instructed to select whisky, sherry and one white and one red wine. Normally Mina was death on the demon drink, this WAS pushing the boat out! You'd think it was Charles and Camilla that was coming.

My mother gave me enough money to nip back down the street for a new top, sandals and a skirt in case the Americans were offended by the sight of a teenager in jeans and trainers. Last port of call was the butchers where a list was left of what was to be delivered fresh on the Saturday. There had to be plenty black pudding, a Willie-Douglas favourite. No problem there – the place was sort of famous for its marag dhubh which to me was quite disgusting when you stopped to think.

The visitors arrived late Saturday afternoon. Flag had a bit of a face on him, I heard after that the American woman thought he was the 'shaffoor' and had offered him a tip. He took it too – quite right.

W.D. was smart in a dark suit spoiled by the addition of a bright yellow tartan waistcoat. He had a very loud voice, perhaps from talking over the noise of car engines. The wife, Melanie, was introduced. She was quite small, dressed and made up to the nines and wearing a pair of fancy purple glasses like you'd see on Dame Edna Everage. She didn't bother taking off her gloves before shaking hands which I thought was quite rude nor was there a trace of a smile as she surveyed her husband's original home. I saw her brush an imaginary speck of something from the seat before lowering herself cautiously and I was sorry now that we'd banished Scooty the cat; he'd have made straight for her elegant lap.

After a bit my mother started getting tea things ready while Auntie Mina showed them through to the bedroom saying she'd give them a minute to settle in. Flag had already taken off at high speed. I heard Melanie bleating something about 'ongsweet'. For devilment I

51

thought of offering her the old under-the-bed 'po' which we still had out in the shed. Even with me standing there she whined on … the bed was hard, she was allergic to Asiatic lilies and, I saw her shudder – no way was she going to step onto the sheepskin rug which had been specially bought along with a new mat for in front of the sitting room fire. The old mat had a big burn where a peat had fallen out. Biting my tongue I left them to it, hoping sincerely that Willie-D had the gumption to point out all his mother had done to make them welcome or was the loud voice a cover for him being a spineless lump.

A while later when I was opening a tin for Scooty, a rare treat – he was used to scraps, I heard my mother and Mina discussing what had clearly become a situation. Mina was upset, my mother soothing and cross at the same time. How dare this tarted-up American madam be so dismissive of the hospitality offered! They were to stay just one night then get a hotel in town, not easy at this time of year and worse still on a Sunday. The atmosphere round the table was somewhat strained. Melanie had latterly announced she was a vegetarian but had grudgingly agreed to accept a cheese and mushroom omelette.

That afternoon I had made a pretty table centrepiece from heather and myrtle interwoven with bog cotton and other machair plants. I'd even threaded in a bit of tartan ribbon. In the silence which followed saying grace I noticed a small black crawly thing fall from among the flowers and scuttle across the snowy white cloth. I watched in fascination as it climbed up the edge of Melanie's plate and vanished among the chopped lettuce leaves which garnished the dish.

The omelette was actually approved and seeing how everyone else was enjoying their black pudding with such relish she agreed to give it a go. I watched her prong a forkful into her dainty mouth and almost slid off my chair to keep from laughing. So much for vegetarian . . .

Later on I would take great delight in telling her exactly what went into the making of a marag.

On the Spur of the Moment

'This net screen could do with a wash,' thought Chrisanne, watching from behind it to spot the town service bus when it came round the corner past Norrie's Garage. This gave her time to do up the buttons of her shabby tweed coat and knot her headscarf firmly beneath her chin. Chrisanne checked that her purse was in the big shopping bag before closing and locking the Manse's front door. There were glimpses of sun among the scudding clouds and a lark sang as it soared the skies. The agreeable scent of newly cut grass filled the air. Kenny Grant had the mower going behind the hardy Fergie tractor whose peeling grey paintwork and dented mudguards bore witness to many years' service.

With a brief blink of its orange indicator the bus slowed towards her and stopped to let the door hiss open.

"Good morning Mistress MacIntyre," Donnie Diesel greeted her from behind the steering wheel. "Nice weather isn't it. And how are you today?"

"Yes it's a grand day indeed. I'm fine thanks. How's yourself these days?"

"Can't complain really; still a bit bothered with my back now and again – probably with sitting in this seat so much. You'll be off up the town then?"

"Just that Donnie. I felt like a day out and I've a wee parcel to post."

This insignificant information was better offered rather than prised from her question by question. She took her ticket and her change and sat down. There were few passengers. She only recognised Trawler Dan nodding off in a seat near the back. After a lifetime at the fishing he liked to go to the Mission for the crack with the other old worthies.

Far in the distance the rippling sea glistened. As the bus rattled its way along the single track road Chrisanne looked out at the blue expanse and wondered again how long it would be before they could have that promised trip to the mainland. Her sister in Inverness kept an open invitation to visit. If only her husband wasn't so tied to his work and so reluctant to be away from his parish, Chrisanne sighed.

She felt as though life was passing her by with her fortieth birthday not that many years away.

Sheep grazed nonchalantly right up to the narrow grass verges, bolder ones lay down on the tarred surface as if it was provided for their comfort. Amused by this rural idiosyncrasy summer visitors stopped to take photos but lorry drivers on their way to the ferry blasted air horns and directed expletives at unperturbed fleecy backs.

There was the usual mid-morning queue in the Post Office. One 'position closed' sign was up behind the protective glass. Her turn came, the parcel was weighed and exclaimed over.

"Oh Australia is it? A long way to go indeed."

Catriona Mhór at the counter was just about as nosy as Donnie Diesel on the bus.

"Yes," offered Chrisanne. "It's to my niece for her fifteenth birthday. A Fair Isle cardigan. I knitted it myself."

"Isn't that grand? She will be pleased; just the thing for the cold weather." Catriona went on in her homely way, attaching the required stamps with great precision. Chrisanne nodded and smiled to people in the line as she made her way to the exit.

Walking toward the main shopping area she noticed there was a bit of a stir outside what used to be the Hydro Board showroom. It had stood empty for several months following re-location to the edge of town retail park and speculation as to its eventual new occupancy had been rife. Suggestions had included pet shop, computer sales, furniture store or yet another Estate Agents. Others with long faced pessimism predicted the infiltration of betting shops or one of these modern places selling unmentionable things to the depraved and immoral.

Chrisanne crossed the street to get a better look. Above the façade an artistically-lettered sign proclaimed 'Head to Toe…Fashion and Beauty.' In the wide window the modishly clad mannequins in elaborately posed positions were almost obscured by posters and banners and little coloured flags. She went over for a closer look.

'GRAND OPENING!!   Special offers this week only!! Complete make-over!! Be the first!! Buy One Get One Free!! Don't be shy Ladies, COME ON IN!!'

And rather to her surprise Chrisanne took the spur of the moment decision to do just that.

The interior was a welcoming haven of subdued lighting and subtle perfume. She saw soft seating, low tables with magazines and brochures and pale pink walls displaying photographs of elegantly coiffed heads. Alongside, various framed certificates declared the expertise and achievement of the workers therein. Soothing music oozed from invisible speakers. The whole relaxed atmosphere was designed to lure the undecided to a world far from household chores and family obligations.

Chrisanne allowed herself to be led through by a smiling young assistant attired in a pink nylon smock above sleek black trousers. The next few hours drifted past in blissful tranquillity. Her unruly hair was shampooed and styled and streaked with blond highlights. She had her first-ever leg wax, her feet were massaged and manipulated and her hands deftly manicured, though Chrisanne had some doubts about the bright blue nail colour. Her face had been cleansed and toned and made up in a way that even she agreed took years off her.

Thinking it would be a pity not to complete the new look with some smarter clothes Chrisanne had again offered up her seldom used credit card and invested in a plain navy three-quarter length linen-look jacket along with a neat skirt in a toning shade of blue. It had small pleats front and back and was a whole lot shorter than she was in the way of wearing. The frill-necked beige blouse would 'go with anything' the sales girl had enthused. Her new shoes had a modest heel – Chrisanne felt some attention should be paid to the practicalities of rural life.

She walked to the bus stop with the cast-off clothing in her big bag.

Donnie Diesel's face was a picture as she climbed on board.

"Great heavens Mistress MacIntyre. I hardly knew a bit of you." He laughed. "Wait till your husband sees you – he'll think he has a new woman."

Chrisanne took her seat, tugging ineffectually at the skirt which barely covered her knees. She was aware of the waft of the heady perfume she'd been sprayed with at the last minute and was glad when the bus reached her road end.

In the house opposite Peigi MacSween was setting the table for supper.

"Would you come and look at this," she called to her sister Dolina in the kitchen. "Some painted hussy is away up to the MacIntyres. She's got a huge bag of something with her."

Dollag came through, nodding her head sagely. "She'll be in trouble of some sort, mark my words. Chrisanne will soon put her right."

Back in her own kitchen Chrisanne was guiltily realising that there was not enough time to prepare and cook the liver and bacon she had mentioned to her husband before he left for Rhynagol that morning. He'd be back any minute now and would have to make do with quiche and a salad instead. She heard the car coming up the gravel drive as she was putting water in the kettle.

The Reverend Iain MacIntyre climbed wearily from his old Ford Orion, pondering sadly on the lack of moral fibre of the couple at whose marriage he had officiated and at the same time eagerly anticipating the tasty supper which awaited. He placed his black hat and his well-used Bible on the hall table and went through to greet his wife . . .

Out of the Frying Pan . . .

Thankful to be home, the Reverend Iain MacIntyre went through to the kitchen.

"Good afternoon," he said courteously, not recognising the woman standing at the sink. He observed that there were some dishes on the table but failed to discern any fine cooking smells.

Chrisanne turned with a nervous smile. "Oh you're home dear. Did the day go well for you?" She was washing lettuce under the cold tap. The Minister drew in a deep breath, his complexion turning a worrying shade of purple.

"Did the day go well for me?" he repeated with a face like a gathering storm.

"I have just heard the holy marriage vows of a couple whose child may well be born before the end of this month. I endured the indifferent meal seated next to an aunt of the groom who seemed to be wearing someone else's dentures and could only talk about her various operations. Afterwards I drove back for miles at a crawl behind a campervan the size of a small bus whose occupants' lack of consideration and scant understanding of the use of passing places obliged me to overlook the Good Book's teaching that the meek shall inherit the earth. It took several blasts of the horn before they drew in and waved me on . . . and then I come in here to find my wife painted and scented like the Whore of Babylon and you have the audacity to ask about my day! What may I ask has been going on in yours?"

Chrisanne began wrapping the lettuce leaves in a clean tea-towel, her mind in a fluster. With her husband in his present humour she realised that a brief and light-hearted explanation was not likely to suffice, so she merely said that she'd had a day in town, with the parcel, and had taken the opportunity to spruce herself up a bit.

"I paid for it all out of my own money," she added defiantly. "Where's the harm in that?"

"Did you stop to consider what people would say?" Rev. MacIntyre was furious now. "You have a position to be aware of in this place and I do not wish to be made a laughing stock. I suggest you do something about it right now!"

He banged his fist on the table, rattling the crockery Chrisanne had hastily set out. She turned from his disapproving glare and walked out to the lobby, feeling brave enough to remind him that they were in fact living in the 21st century but not daring to wait for a response.

Instead of going upstairs she followed a second spur of the moment impulse which took her out the front door and along the path, past the field with its waterproof-wrapped silage bales to the croft of her friend Annie Grant. Annie and her brother Kenny were in the cosy kitchen with Emmerdale on the TV. She was welcomed in and Annie bustled to get the kettle on, scarcely concealing her curiosity as she exclaimed over Chrisanne's transformed appearance. Kenny eyed her appraisingly as well.

"My you do look glamorous," he grinned as he lifted over a chair for her. He had long since nursed a soft spot for his pretty neighbour and considered her 'wasted' on that dull and cheerless man she was married to.

"Thanks Kenny." Chrisanne looked up, noticing how brown his face and arms were after all his outdoor work.

"Well, where do you want me to start?" she asked teasingly, relaxed now among friends.

Finding that the rumbling pangs of hunger were beginning to outweigh his irritation the minister took a look about for signs of anything edible. It was clear that nothing had been prepared. Hadn't Chrisanne mentioned liver and bacon before he set off for Rhynagol that morning? Sure enough, the fridge disclosed a cling-filmed plate of the town butcher's best liver and next to it a pack of supermarket rashers. After some door-opening and drawer-pulling he found a frying pan into which he poured a generous measure of cooking oil, turning the nearest ring on to full heat. Selecting a sharp blade from the rack he made short work of slicing the liver into manageable pieces, blissfully unaware of the unsightly scars he was leaving on the worktop surface. He tossed the bits as they were into the smoking hot fat which hissed and spluttered, stinging the backs of his hands with burning droplets. Somewhat too hot, he decided, turning the knob to low and giving the pan a shake. The liver was welded firmly to its non-stick base. Using the same knife he prised loose the slices and turned them over. They neither looked nor smelled very appetising.

'I'll do better with the bacon,' he promised himself, selecting another pan and reluctantly regretting his earlier outburst. Chrisanne should be here, going about things in her quietly expert way. He had been out of order in his rapid judgement, he realised, as the bacon sizzled more temperately in the smaller pan. There was so much to deal with in preparing a supper – the kettle had been filled but not switched on. There was only one slice of bread, the butter was still rock hard from the freezer and only the merest scrape of jam remained in the dish. Fighting renewed annoyance he overlooked the need to place a heat-resisting mat beneath the liver's hot pan when he lifted it to the worktop. The smell of melting plastic caught his throat as he stared in dismay at the neatly scorched circle.

The phone's sudden clamour startled him. Wiping his greasy hands on a tea-towel which he snatched from the draining board he hastened to answer, leaving half-dry lettuce leaves strewn over the kitchen floor.

"Hello," he said tersely, then recognised at once the voice of Annie Grant informing him that Chrisanne was at the croft; she was a bit upset (she makes it sound like it was all my fault, glowered the Reverend) but she was thinking about coming home now. Annie had a half pan of mutton stew left. Would they manage to use it up?

Further conversation was halted by the sudden wheeping of the smoke alarm. Muttering a brief thanks the minister replaced the receiver and dashed back to the kitchen. His bacon was burnt as black as the devil's eyebrows. Was ever a man's patience so sorely tested? He flapped the tea-towel vigorously until silence was restored.

"Will I walk over the road with you?" Kenny enquired gallantly.
Chrisanne laughed. "I think not. Thanks all the same. Amn't I in enough bother for one day?"

Annie picked up the torch from the dresser and the two women set off back along the path and into the house where the weary minister had unhitched his stiff white collar and was on his knees on the kitchen floor . . . gathering up bits of soggy lettuce.

Donnie Diesel

The bus rattled over the cattle grid more briskly than it would have done with passengers on board. A busy summer day now winding down, Donald Archibald Montgomery Campbell, known to all as Donnie Diesel, leaned his elbow out of the open window.

'And I'll be in Scotland befooooore you,' he bellowed tunelessly, with Runrig on full volume. He hoped his mother would have herring in oatmeal for supper, with potatoes in their skins, the best meal you could ask for. The cailleach always liked to hear about the on-goings of his day and by jove, did he have something to entertain her with tonight! A strong smell still hung about the bus in spite of the air conditioning blasting and the tops pushed up. He wondered how the minister would have reacted to his new-look wife. She had surely splashed out a small fortune on clothes, not to mention the hair-do and the painted face. He'd had to look twice when he picked her up at the bus stance on her way home, and the waft of perfume could have knocked out an entire shinty team.

"What are we going to do about your birthday?" Donnie asked his mother as they sat back later with their usual mugs of tea. "It's not every day you get to be seventy. Not that you look it," he added considerately.

"Never mind your flattery." Jessie Campbell patted down her springy grey hair. "You know fine I don't want any fuss and none of that daft stuff you see on TV when everyone leaps out from behind the sofa shouting 'surprise! surprise!' I'd turn and run."

"Well, I know for a fact that my bossy sisters have been on the phone a lot. Rhona was telling Katey that she and her friend could have the spare back room with the two beds, so someone must be coming with her from Edinburgh. Perhaps it's a boyfriend. It's been years since that two-timing waster ran out on her."

His mother frowned. It had been a lot to deal with at the time. "Katey seems happy enough as she is – an interesting job in that big library and doing research or whatever it's called for some book she's wanting to write. It was just the bad weather stopped her getting home that Christmas." Jessie rose, gathering the dishes noisily. "She's bringing this woman called Cynthia, another librarian, from Kingstown I believe she said."

"Oh aye, that'll be the place not far from Edinburgh. Another librarian? Not much fun there then." His sister Katey was all sensible shoes and classical music and not much given to frivolity. Och well, he supposed it went with the job. "I expect they will have their noses stuck in books all the time."

"I don't mind what they do," his mother said, "as long as I have family all around me. That would be the best birthday of all. Your sister Rhona will be here with her husband and the children but it's too far for our Angus to come from the States. It's not likely your other brother will make it either, he's a bit under the thumb with that stuck-up madam he married. If I'm lucky I'll get the usual 'bookay' of flowers. But no doubt your Auntie Mina will appear even if it's only out of nosiness."

"She'll be there all right." Donnie grinned, well aware of how difficult his elderly aunt could be – nothing was ever as it should be, or as it was 'in my young day.'

"And what about yourself?" his mother asked. "Thirty five years old and no sign of a wife. I had high hopes for you with that nice young schoolteacher but Jacob MacDonald beat you to it."

"Well, he's a lot better looking than me. He's thinner and he still has his hair." Donnie's own expanding bald spot was a constant source of disappointment. "Shona was just right for him; his wee girl needed someone especially as the granny's getting on a bit. Ach, I might surprise you yet. What size was the slippers again? Wasn't that what you said you'd like?" It was time to shift the conversation away from matrimonial expectations.

The first Saturday in September soon came round. It had rained steadily all day. But when Donnie left the house that morning there had been a stir of activity especially in the kitchen where mother and daughter had started on the baking and cooking. There would likely be enough food to feed the entire village although the old lady still maintained nobody would bother to turn up.

His shift over, Donnie took a detour to the airport before heading for home. Safely wrapped in the boot of his car were the two framed paintings which he had ordered for his mother. One was of heather hills and moorland, the other of waves rolling over the beautiful wide sandy beach where she had played as a girl. The slippers had not been forgotten, the best the shop had to offer in the cheerful red tartan she liked so much.

"I can't wait to see the look on her face," he said as the car turned in towards the croft. Several motors were already parked up and the wheezy notes of Trawler Dan's ancient concertina were barely audible above the chatter of voices.

Donnie opened the room door with a flourish. "Look who I found," he shouted out, ushering his brother Angus into the room. The reactions were just as he expected, astonished looks and welcoming cries. Then the smartly dressed and slightly bemused American wife was introduced as Lucille.

Katey appeared through the kitchen door bearing a splendid white confection. "We never chanced seventy candles," she said with a laugh. "Didn't want to burn the house down. These will be easier to blow out."

Candles in the shape of a seven and a zero flickered daintily on the iced top.

"Hallo at last Donnie. It's good to see you again." She spoke in Gaelic to her brother. "I'd like you to meet my friend Cynthia Banderman; she's started work in the library with me."

Donnie looked across and felt a blush spreading up his face. There was nothing plain and boring about Cynthia Banderman. She was more like a model stepped off a fashion page, slender and smiling and wearing the brightest patterned dress he had ever seen. Her curly black hair was swept upwards with shiny gold clasps and her wrists rattled with bracelets as she reached to shake his hand. At his elbow he heard Auntie Mina sniffing some disapproving comment about 'the look of her.'

Cynthia said how pleased she was to be here on this beautiful Scottish island so different from the one where she had grown up. She thanked them all for their kindness in allowing her to share this special day and said how much she was looking forward to learning more about local traditions and culture.

Joining in the ripple of approval which followed Donnie thought about the tickets he had bought to hear Capercaille play in town next Friday and wondered if Cynthia might be interested in that sort of culture.

Kingston, not Kingstown. It was an easy mistake to make.

The Lights on the Hill

"If you rub that window any longer you'll wear a hole in the glass." Don-Alec called out to his wife as he wiped his feet dutifully on the rubber doormat.

"Och, you know how I like to have everything just so when Eilidh and the boys come. I can hardly remember the last time they were here."

Cathy stood back to check her handiwork. The homely kitchen was filled with the mouth-watering aroma of freshly baked bread and a pot of broth simmered on the stove. "Surely they won't be long now?"

She checked the clock for the umpteenth time. "You know that man of hers is more used to fast motorways than quiet country roads. I just hope he drives safely."

Eilidh had first encountered Willerby Bryce when his family firm of property developers had sent him to the Inverness Estate Agents where she worked. Sourcing Highland properties for sale or lease had been his instruction and Eilidh had been flattered by his courtesy and attention when they drove to inspect possible places in some of the more remote parts of the Highlands. In turn, he claimed to have been bewitched by her gentle Scottish lilt. Willerby had been her first serious 'romance'.

Despite their best efforts her parents had not taken a great liking to the man their youngest daughter had chosen to marry, nor had matters improved with the passing of time. It wasn't because he was from south of the border and from an affluent background; it was more his over-bearing manner and dictatorial ways. His word was law. No wife of his was going to go out to work; a woman's place was in the home bringing up the children. Eilidh had to be content with her beautiful modern house in the city of York where Willerby earned serious amounts of money within his family firm. Harold was now thirteen and his brother Oliver four years younger. It had been a source of quiet disappointment to the grandparents that more traditional family names had been unconditionally rejected.

The sound of an approaching vehicle made the old couple turn their heads simultaneously. Cathy hurriedly tugged off her apron as they watched the enormous Land Cruiser pull up at the gate. Oliver ran excitedly into his Granny's warm embrace while Don-Alec hugged his daughter with a tear in his eye. Somehow the youngest seemed most precious, perhaps because they have been yours for the shortest time.

Calling a brief greeting Willerby opened the boot and began hauling out cases and boxes while Harold stood uncomfortably hesitant, not at all sure if hugs and cuddles were much his scene nowadays. Instead he gravely shook his grandfather's hand then somewhat reluctantly allowed Granny to fold her arms around him as she had always done. Happily reunited, they chatted their way into the house.

"I can't believe how fine the weather has been these last few days," Willerby boomed at breakfast one morning. "And I thought it always rained in the west. Well, I've organised a fishing trip on one of the sea lochs for a couple of days. Harold will be coming with me. No, sorry Oliver, you are much too young and you'd only get in the way."

The boy's crestfallen face brightened as he heard his Grandfather say how he had something special planned for just the two of them next day. "We'll leave Mam and Granny behind. They want to look through some old photographs."

Loaded with fishing gear and camping equipment Willerby and Harold roared away in the four by four after an early breakfast, promising they would keep in touch by phone if they could get a signal. Mother and daughter carried several boxes of stuff down from the attic with much blowing of dust and smiles of anticipation.

"Be off with you then," Cathy prompted her husband. Oliver needed no encouragement. He'd been ready for over an hour in jeans, a thick sweater and the good strong boots he'd been given for his holiday in the wilds. They set off in the direction of Tor Chamais with a rucksack of food and grandfather's folding telescope. The sun shone intermittently and a slight breeze kept them cool as they clambered up the hill, the young and the old happy in each other's company.

Much later in the day with the light fading and the midgies feasting they made their way homeward, Oliver bursting to tell of how they had sighted deer and how an eagle had swooped high above their heads. They had spotted a buzzard on a rock and watched a kestrel hovering over its prey. Grandfather knew all about such things.

"What do you like to do back home in York?" the old man asked. "There won't be a place like this for you to roam about in."

"We never get out much on our own; Daddy says it's too dangerous. He takes us places in the car. We've been to the big museum, Grandfather. It's a super place, all the old trains and railway stuff. There's a huuuge blue engine called Mallard that Daddy says was the fastest steam loco, locomotive ever. And there's the Viking village too – it's really cool. They had big boats with sails. And they had axes."

Oliver stumbled and almost fell over a tussock of grass. As he righted himself he grasped his Grandfather's sleeve and pointed with his other hand.

"Look over there, near the bottom of that hill; can you see some lights flickering? They've gone out now. No, I see them again. Is that somebody's house?"

Don-Alec felt as if a cold finger had touched the back of his neck. "Nobody there now son," he replied. "That was where a man called Calum Gillies lived; he worked on the ferry in his young day."

Don-Alec was reluctant to tell the tale of what happened to the poor old man a lot of years ago. He had gone to the shore one night in a fearful storm to try and help the folk from a cruiser-type boat that was dashed onto the rocks. The effort had been too much for old Calum and he had died exhausted where he fell. A young boy had been the only survivor. Calum's dog had stayed with him till the coastguard came searching.

Neither did Don-Alec want to mention that he had himself at the time witnessed these strange lights on the other side of the hill and that old Highland superstition believed them to be a foreboding of disaster. He prayed inwardly that his innocent young grandson had not inherited the gift of the 'sight' which in truth was more like a curse. Swallowing hard, he began to play a guessing game with Oliver about what they thought might be for supper.

Unlike at home the two boys shared a bedroom here on holiday and Oliver had to admit that he did miss Harold … but only just a little.

'At least he is not here to make fun of Bertie,' he thought, snuggling beneath the covers with his one-eared teddy.

He woke just after seven next morning, hearing a car coming up the road. Perhaps Daddy and Harold had come back early, Oliver wondered as he climbed out of the bed and peered through the window.

The car was stopped and a young policeman got out, putting on his cap with a very solemn expression before raising his hand to knock on the door.

Breaking the News

'They don't prepare you for this in training,' he thought, locking the car behind him. Young, thin, new to the job, he tugged his tunic jacket straight, took a calming breath and knocked on the door. Inside a dog barked. A man's voice admonished it in Gaelic. The door opened.

"Good morning Sir. Mr. MacAskill is it?" The man nodded, his expression concerned.

"I'm Police Constable David Souter. I'm sorry; I need to have a word. Would you mind if . . ."

"Come in, come in, just through here," Don-Alec opened an inner door which led into the sitting room.

"It may be bad news I'm afraid. There was an upturned boat spotted floating out on Loch Achill, the young lady who drives the taxi reported it. You'll know her, Miss Evelyn Fraser? A silver Toyota Land Cruiser was parked on rough ground a short way off the road." He read out a registration number.

Don-Alec looked up. "That's my son-in-law's car; he's up on holiday from England. They went off yesterday for some fishing."

"I'm really sorry Sir; would he be a man in his late forties perhaps, stocky build? Two bodies were found . . ." God, this was the worst bit. He swallowed. "Was there a young boy with him?"

"Yes, yes, my grandson Harold." Don-Alec gripped the back of a chair. "What on earth could have come over them? It wasn't a wild day."

"It seems neither of them was wearing life-jackets." PC.Souter went on.

Don-Alec felt a surge of anger. How typically arrogant of Bryce to think anything like that would be necessary.

The door opened and Mrs MacAskill appeared. The front of her green blouse was buttoned up all wrong, her feet shoved into worn slippers.

"Has something happened?" She looked anxiously at her husband. Don-Alec led her to a seat and broke the news as gently as he could. Constable Souter turned aside to give them a private moment. The old woman's face turned pale.

"No, no that can't be true," she whimpered. "Not little Harold, the poor soul. AND his father? Eilidh will have to be told."

Cathy struggled against tears, time for that later when the awful news had sunk in.

The door opened again.

"Eilidh will have to be told what?" She gaped at the man in uniform, dreading the worst. "It's Harold isn't it? And Willerby. What's happened? Are they all right?" Her voice was barely a whisper. She swayed where she stood.

Her mother caught her arm gently. "Come through to the kitchen a'ghràidh. I'll put the kettle on and I'll explain."

As the two women left the room the older one turned and thanked the policeman.

"This could not have been easy for you," she said sympathetically. The lad was scarcely much older than Harold.. Harold . . . she felt her eyes fill with tears at the thought of the grandson she would never see again.

"There will have to be a formal identification." PC. Souter consulted his notebook again. Your daughter . . . Mrs. Bryce . . . do you think she'd be up to it? It's all been such a shock."

"You can leave that to me." Don-Alec was firm. Truth be known he had never found Willerby easy to get on with but he certainly didn't deserve this untimely death. And as for Harold! He couldn't bear to think.

"Will it be all right if I phone the Station later to arrange a time?"

"Of course, Sir. You just let us know when you feel ready." He folded his notebook into the top pocket of his tunic and picked up his cap from the table. "I'll be on my way then. I am truly sorry for your loss."

Don-Alec showed him out.

As he turned from the door he saw Oliver standing at the top of the stairs holding his much-loved teddy by one leg.

"I saw a policeman Grandfather. Did we do something bad? Can I get dressed now? Will I need my boots today?"

Setting his face in a smile Don-Alec climbed towards him. He picked up Oliver and Bertie and carried them gently into the boys' bedroom.

Glad to have the worst part of his day over, PC Souter drove thoughtfully down the narrow road, amazing over the dignified resilience he had just witnessed. He slowed down over the bridge and indicated left towards the town.

Thy Will Be Done

"So long as you are breaking bread beneath my roof you will have the courtesy to respect my wishes."

The minute he came through the kitchen door Duncan knew he was in for it again. He tried to avoid his father's reproachful gaze.

"Where have you been? Why were you not home before the Sabbath began? What have you got to say for yourself?"

Willie John Morrison was already respectably attired in his dark Sunday suit. He was shaved and what hair he had left was neatly combed over awaiting the addition of his best cap.

"Och you know what it's like Father, I had a drop too much to drink so I stayed up in town with uh … a friend. Better that than chance driving back."

You'd expect the old man to be pleased with such good sense, he thought. But no, no, the observance of the Sabbath Day came before all else. He clattered the car keys defiantly onto the wooden table.

"Just give me a minute," Duncan called over his shoulder on the way to the bathroom. "I'll come to church with you." Better get on the bodach's good side. There was a long way to go yet if he was ever going to bring him round to the ideas he had for the croft. His father was proving very resistant to change. Such matters would not be discussed on this holy day.

Duncan splashed cold water over his face and dried himself roughly on the towel. Dragging a comb through his hair he went back into the kitchen and took the keys from the table.

"You could at least put on a tie," grumbled the father. "And we will walk to the House of God on our own good legs."

Donald Macleod was presiding over the plate as they entered the church vestibule, agreeing about the weather in his subdued Sunday voice while they presented their offerings. Willie John led the way in then stood aside at the end of the family pew to allow his son to pass. Duncan sidled into the seat which had once held seven. He hoped he could keep awake after the heavy night.

Lachlan MacKenzie was putting out the line today, leading the worshippers in the timeless tradition of unaccompanied psalm singing, unscripted and unhurried. Above him in the pulpit the Reverend Lachlan Mackenzie senior waited quietly to address his congregation.

"Your Aunt Isa is a grand cook," said Willie John as father and son later made their way back up Pier Road. After church Willie John's sister usually had dinner for them in her own house down by the quayside. There had been the promise of a pan of soup and a mince pie she would bring round at the start of the week. "Mind you, so was your mother, God rest her soul. There was no-one to beat her at the baking."

Duncan could tell from his father's voice that his loss was still hard to bear. "Never mind Dad haven't you still got me here," he said, trying to lighten the mood. "We're doing all right with the fry-ups and the microwave dinners."

"I'm not that keen on these new-fangled contraptions," muttered the old man. "I know full well that your sister Marianne would have stayed on to see to us after we lost your mother but I did not want her training to go to waste. Many's the one in that big hospital will have been glad of her care. And as for Kirsty and thon useless lump she married, they are well out of it living the high life in Manitoba."

"And aren't my brothers doing fine as well," Duncan added. He thought about the scholarly John, headmaster of a City school and Donald Angus, the youngest of the family, involved in a project to bring clean water to some drought stricken part of Africa. "Perhaps I should have been a doctor!" he suggested. Both of them chuckled at the absurdity of this notion. Duncan's contact with schooling had barely covered the legal requirements. It had suited him better to be working on the croft at the potatoes or the peats or helping with the lambing and the gathering. In his early twenties decent wages were to be had when the fabrication yard started up. He was home between shifts and on days off. Now the yard was awaiting decisions regarding its future, the workforce laid off. With the boredom of a Sunday afternoon looming ahead Duncan thought he'd take the dogs for a long walk on the sands and leave his father in quiet contemplation.

"Would you look at the day that's in it!" Willie John exclaimed the following morning. The sheep had to be rounded up from their hillside grazings and brought down to the fank whatever the weather.

"Have you seen that form I had for posting, it was there on Friday?" Willie John rummaged through the sideboard drawer.

71

"It's on the mantelpiece behind that photo," Duncan pointed out. "You're as stubborn as a wet peat Dad. When are you going to see about better glasses? There's a fine new place opened up in town last March, not far from the Co-op."

"There's nothing wrong with my glasses," argued the old man. "They've done me fine for the past ten years. Maybe they could do with a wee wipe." He reached for the kitchen towel.

"I'll take you there by force some day if I have to," Duncan threatened jokingly. "You know fine well that your eyesight is not as good as it was. And an old fellow like yourself gets an eye test for nothing."

With the collies at their heels the men took the path to meet neighbours who were helping with the gathering. Duncan thought it was worth a try.

"Stop here a minute Dad," he began. "Think what this place could look like on a fine summer day if there was a couple of chalets between here and the fank, and a bit levelled out for a caravan or two. Plenty of people would come. They'd love it here and they would pay good money." Duncan's words came out in a rush.

"Watch what you're doing with that stick!" His father's sudden shake of the fist had brought the cromag near to collision with Duncan's head.

"Do you know how long Morrisons have worked this land?" Willie John asked crossly. "You'd want to see it turned into a playground for loud mouthed Americans and the idle Sassennach? Aren't we doing fine with the crop and the sheep and the cows?"

"The red cow is so worn done that we had to lift the last calf from out of her; have you forgotten that? The tractor is knackered, the byre roof leaks like a strainer and where will the money come from to sort all that?"

"The same place it would come from for all your fancy ideas."

Willie John's usually placid voice rose to an angry shout. "Just forget about all your modern notions and get on with the job in hand." He stomped off, shaking his head.

"Well, well if that's the way it is to be." Duncan was not to be bested. "Perhaps it's time I got back to Exxon; they had notices out for off shore jobs. I could be out there on a drilling rig or a platform doing my shifts and getting on with my life, and nobody to say stop now lads it's coming up to the Sabbath day."

"Do what you want. You usually do anyway." They walked on in silence.

The dreich weather continued for days with drenching rain and finger-numbing wind. Duncan and his father worked among the sheep, dosing, checking ear tags and hooves and clipping away chunks of matted fleece. Nothing more was said about making any changes, Willie John confident that his word was to be heeded, Duncan anxious to dispel any lingering animosity.

By Friday they had finished mending the fence in the bottom field where a rotting corner post had collapsed, taking yards of netting with it. After the two men changed out of their dirty overalls the last of Isa's mince pie and a panful of their own potatoes made a satisfying supper. Duncan had second go of the bathroom. His father said he always took far too long preening himself for the weekend. He was coming down the stairs when he heard the front door scrape open and recognised his aunt's voice speaking to the collies.

"Are you off out then?" Isa wanted to know. She'd come for her soup pan. "Here's a bit of beef stew I thought would do you for Saturday." Duncan could feel the good smell of it coming from below the lid.

"I don't know what we'd do without you." Duncan smiled fondly, taking the dish from her hands. His hair was spiked up and the leather jacket was slung over one shoulder.

"Fergie's playing at Laxdale. Is that where you're heading?" Isa well remembered her own dancing days when the Strip the Willow would have you near off your feet and the band would play till daybreak.

"Not the night Auntie," he replied. "Stacey isn't keen on that sort of stuff. She wants to go to the disco in town." Duncan well knew the opinion his family had of his city girlfriend with her purple lips and nails and bits of skirts.

"Well that doesn't surprise me. If you had still been seeing Mairi Ross you could have gone to a proper dance with proper music and not that disco racket. And where's your father tonight anyway?"

"Off to the Community Centre. They're wanting to make a garden out of that bit of rough ground and there's a committee getting set up to try and start things off. They want to get in touch with these lads from the TV programme."

73

Isa was heading for the door.

"Do you want a lift back?" offered Duncan "It's on my road anyway."

"No. Thanks all the same. It's a fine night. That perfume coming off you is making me dizzy." Duncan admitted he might have overdone the aftershave a bit.

"Oidhche mhàth," Isa called from the lobby.

Duncan banked the fire with dross, ordered the dogs outside and took care locking the front door. He drove slowly past the old woman on the track then gunned the GTi in the direction of the town as soon as he swung onto the hard road. It was the devil's own job finding somewhere to park on a Friday night.

Turnaround

"I've had just about enough of that noise." Duncan helped Stacey teeter down the steps as the crowd spilled out from the disco.

"You're getting too old," she teased, "and I'm gasping for a fag." She found the packet in the depths of a cluttered bag. "See that young DJ? Him wi' the ginger hair; I could have got off with him you know – he kept giving me the eye."

"Maybe you should have." Duncan was not in the best of humour. "And I'm telling you again, I do not want to go back to the flat tonight when your pals have that desperate crowd of lassies up from Glasgow. I'm going home to the croft whether you like it or not Why do you think I've kept off the drink all this time?"

"That's fine with me," Stacey hiccupped as she ground out her cigarette end. "I'll just come with you; you've got a carry-out haven't you?"

Duncan looked at her. At times he wondered if he was going off her a bit. She was the life and soul of any party and fair game for a good time but not someone he could see a future with.

"Are you sure? You know the score there. The old man won't like it. It will definitely be the spare room for you. And there's nothing wrong with his ears."

"Stop being such an old spoil sport. We'll manage something." Stacey was already heading for the passenger door of the Golf. "Put on some music and none of your teuchter rubbish."

Obligingly he pushed a CD into the slot and let the Gallagher brothers do their stuff.

Duncan was surprised to see there was no light on in the porch when they pulled up at the front door. Both dogs rose to meet him from the shelter of the peat stack. It was not like his father to leave them outside. He went in ahead of Stacey expecting to find his old man asleep in the chair oblivious to the passing of time. The fire was down and the room was chilly. Duncan took the stairs two at a time and quietly opened the door of his father's room. His bed was empty. Concerned now, Duncan bounded back down the stair.

"There's neither sight nor sign of Father," he said briefly to Stacey who yawned noisily and stretched her arms letting her skimpy blouse reveal an expanse of fake-tanned skin.

"I'm off for a look round the sheds and the yard," he informed her as she selected a bottle of lager from the carrier bag.

"Okey Dokey honey, see you later . . . don't be long . . ." her words were slurring.

Aided by a powerful torch and the two dogs Duncan checked out every corner of the buildings and round the perimeter of their fields. He knew his father's eyesight was not what it had been and he feared that some wrong-footed stumble could have resulted in a fall. Most of their land sloped gently into machair but farther along were cliffs and a steep drop.

Back in the croft kitchen Stacey was sprawled on the couch with a couple of empty bottles at her feet. She stubbed out a cigarette and aimed the butt carelessly at the fireplace.

"What do you think you're doing?" Duncan was annoyed. "You know damn fine the old man hates folk smoking in here. I'm not too keen on it myself."

"No need for all that fuss; can't you open the window? Come on, grab a bottle and give me a cuddle here," she coughed through the cigarette haze.

Duncan glared. "What if something's happened to the old fellow?"

Stacey lurched unsteadily onto her feet and leaned towards him. "Well, if it has, you'll be able to do a' the things you are aye going on about, you know, the caravans and stuff."

Duncan turned to her angrily. "You really are a selfish hard hearted bitch. I don't know what I ever saw in you. Here's twenty quid, phone yourself a taxi and clear off away out of here." He punched a number on his own mobile.

"Is that yourself Kenny? It's Duncan Morrison here. There's no sign of Father home from that committee meeting. Have you any idea where he might be? What? He was never there? Are you sure? That's where he said he was going. I'm just new back from the town. Oh aye, please Kenny, that would be grand. I'll see you and the others down by the fank. We'll work out a plan from there."

With torch beams searching the darkness some folk went to the moor, some to the shore and one or two of the women called from house to house. Mairi Ross was among them, her heart heavy for what the outcome of the night might be. She was very fond of old Mr

Morrison. Nor had Duncan been far from her thoughts in spite of his abrupt rejection.

Daylight crept in and still no trace had been found. The searchers sipped a warming drink in the croft kitchen which to Duncan's relief was empty on their return. It didn't matter that his carryout had gone as well. His face was etched with anxiety and guilt.

"I was quite nasty to him the other day, threatening to go offshore if he didn't let me do things my way. And now, if anything's happened to him it will be all my fault."

The sudden sound of the telephone startled them. Duncan picked it up.

"Oh, madainn mhath. Is that you Isa? Have you any news? You have? He is? Eddie's bringing him? Thank God for that, whatever was he thinking about . . ."

They heard a car stopping. Willie John walked in followed by the driver. Mairi ushered the old man gently into his chair while Kenny poured a dram.

"Where were you? What happened? You had us all worried sick." It was Duncan's turn to ask the questions.

"Och well," began the bodach, unashamedly unapologetic. "You see, it was such a fine night and I got to thinking about all the things that have been said lately. Instead of the meeting I went down to the old sail loft beyond Isa's house. Myself and her Murdo used to sit up there for hours on an old sofa staring out to sea and putting the world to rights. I must have dozed off and the light was coming in when I stirred myself. Stiff as a board I was too."

"We never looked there; Isa said the key had been lost since years." Duncan broke in.

"Maybe hers was but I still kept mine," explained Willie John. "Didn't I come across it in the drawer the day I was looking for thon form. Pour us another wee dram then we'll have a bite of breakfast."

Mairi was already busy in the scullery recalling easily where pans and cups were kept. Bacon and sausages were soon sizzling.

Duncan thanked everyone for their help as they took their leave. They all said it was nothing.

On the Wednesday after all the commotion Willie John was with Isa in the kitchen looking out a tin for the scones she had brought. He heard something coming up the track. It sounded like a motorbike.

Duncan strode in, jangling a set of keys and looking very pleased with himself. "Come on till I show you this," he said, waving his father outside.

"And what may I ask have you got there?" The old man peered forward.

"That," grinned Duncan, "is a quad bike. It can take you anywhere you like, up the hill, across the moor, even over boggy ground. It's easy to learn and it will save a lot of walking. Norrie from the garage said it might take a while till the tractor is fixed. He had a couple of these out in front beside the pumps so I just bought this one."

"Show me how it works." Willie John plumped himself onto the seat.

"Ah, but just you wait a minute," said Duncan. "Whether it pleases you or not, there is one condition before you get to go anywhere. I've made an appointment for you with the optician next Monday. There will be no driving for you boy until you get that new glasses."

One-Way Ticket

"My father warned me about you all these years ago." Kirsty closed the dishwasher door with a satisfying thud. "How often do you think I wish I had listened?"

"Don't give me that." Bobby Neilsen exhaled a thin stream of cigarette smoke. He knew how much it annoyed the hell out of his wife. "You were keen enough to get away back then." He mimicked her Highland accent, 'It's so boring here, I want to see a bit of the wurrruld. Canada sounds really exciting'... you never stopped whining on."

"Probably I meant it at the time. It was hard for me to live up to what my older sister had achieved; they were always saying how well she had done."

"She was the brainy one wasn't she? Never had a boyfriend. I often wondered about her." He laughed derisively.

"And she was starting a wonderful career in nursing," Kirsty added ruefully. "And what was I? Slave labour in that clothes shop, letting out seams and taking up hems and having that awful old Mrs MacGillivray watching every move I made. Anything would have been better than that."

"Huh, is that all I was, a one-way ticket to a better life? Don't make me laugh; you couldn't get enough of me, sneaking around when they'd all gone to church. Your old man got real worked up about the hellfire and eternal damnation that was waiting for you." Bobby grinned at the memory. "Willie John was convinced that I was the spawn of Satan come to lead his daughter astray. Then you had the nerve to go through with a white wedding. You even had me wearing a goddam kilt."

Kirsty picked up a photo in its silver frame. "It never bothered you how hard it was when Matthew was born. Neither your mom or your giddy sister lent a hand at all when I needed it most. Then I had to go back to work real quick; you weren't bringing in a single dollar. Sofeena from across the road was a lifesaver in spite of your insults about her not being one of us."

"How was I supposed to get a job with a mass of dermatitis and a strained back?" Bobby Neilsen shook another cigarette from the pack.

"You could have helped in the house instead of spending hours on the couch switching TV channels and swilling beer and expecting food to appear."

"Damned if I was going to do women's work. It's a wife's place to look after her husband, keep him happy. I know a few others who wouldn't have said no to me turning up on their porch step."

"And what about when Dallas came along, your own daughter and you could hardly bear to look at her after we were told she'd always be slow besides the other kids."

"Yeah, I did feel a bit bad about that, but look at her now. She's never no trouble."

"She was just little when her Grandma Morrison died back home on the island. You knew I wanted to go to my own mother's funeral but no, no way were you going to look after the kids all on your own. There wasn't money for a minder and your sister was on that tour with the Bracknell Brothers thinking she was the next best thing to Dolly Parton."

"I'm getting the hell outa here if all you can do is criticise. Don't know when I'll be back." Bobby snatched up his jacket.

Kirsty folded some newly ironed clothing into neat piles.

"You suit yourself; see if I'm bothered. And I'll tell you something right now buster. Remember that invitation to my brother Duncan's wedding? The one you made me turn down. I'm not letting you spoil anything this time. I've been putting a bit aside for some time and I got a good price for my Grandmother's amethyst brooch and her rings, the ones my mother, God rest her, insisted should be mine. I'm taking the kids home to Scotland. There's flights booked for the middle of next week. And this time it definitely will be a one-way ticket.

Step we Gaily . . .

There were only three days left to wait. Mairi Ross closed the wardrobe door firmly; she was not going to look at the perfect white creation again until Friday. Hanging next to it was the cornflower-blue bridesmaid's dress that her seventeen year old sister Donna had been coaxed to wear.

Katy-Mary Ross had taken great pleasure in choosing her Mother of the Bride outfit, an oatmeal-coloured two piece which would also be fine for wearing to church in the warmer days. Such a pity, she had thought, that the groom's mother was no longer with them. She would have been so proud of Duncan.

Over on the Morrison croft Willie John shared the same thought. Cathy had fought her illness bravely to the last. Never a day went by that he didn't think of her. His sister Isa had done so much for him and the boy over the years and thanks to her good organising the two of them would be smartly togged out for the big day, Willie John in his new navy blue suit and his son in full Highland rig in a Morrison tartan.

And to have nearly all the family home for the occasion, his heart swelled with pride. They had done so well for themselves – Marianne a senior nurse, John the Book, as they called his eldest son, headmaster of a city school and Donald Angus, youngest of them all, overseeing some well-building programme in the Sudan. Sadly daughter Kirsty over in Manitoba had declined the invitation saying her husband's work was too important for him to get away. Willie John had treated this information with scornful disbelief. They had never heard of Bobby Neilsen having anything other than the most casual of employment. The old man often wondered did Kirsty ever regret ignoring her parents' doubts and warnings. But it would be Duncan and Mairi's wedding day on Friday and he couldn't ask for a better daughter in law.

After the solemn church ceremony the young couple were driven to the refurbished Community Hall by Evie Fraser, in the Garage's elderly cream-coloured Rolls Royce. In accordance with modern health and safety regulations outside caterers had been hired, the meal had been marvelled at. Speeches and toasts followed and the company chatted in anticipation of the dancing which would follow.

Roddy William and the Blackhouse Ceilidh Band were getting set up on stage.

Their shop door bearing a sign, 'Closed for family reasons but enquiries may be made at Village Hall', Dolina and Peigi MacSween sat back in their unaccustomed finery in seats where a good eye could be kept on the proceedings. Dollag's shoes pinched a bit, adding to her normally strained look of disapproval. The food was first in the critical list. Potatoes not salted enough, the chicken was tasteless, there were strange under-cooked vegetables and even stranger puddings.

"In the old days," Peigi remarked, "the women would have done it all themselves, getting the chickens ready, making pots of broth and a fine steamed dumpling to finish off with."

"I never had my food on a square plate before this day," Dollag added, "and there was an awful lot of drink on offer from the minute we came through the door. It was just to be sociable that I took that small glass of sherry."

The accordionist squeezed an introductory chord then the band struck up with 'Ho ro my nut brown maiden.' Bride and groom made the traditional first circuit of the floor, Duncan embarrassedly indicating that others should join them.

"They make a lovely couple," Dollag observed. "He looks well in the kilt. Mairi will be good for him; far better than that strumpet from Glasgow he used to hang about with. Remember the time Willie John went missing? It was after that he got back together with Mairi Ross."

Further comments on various family members were made behind discreet hands. John the Book's wife had nothing to be so high and mighty about – wasn't her father a keeper from Coigach? And the other brother had brought a foreign woman, African by the look of her.

"I didn't think much of Eachainn Ross's speech; you'd think the father of the bride would have more to say?" Dollag loved to find fault.

"Och the poor man was a nervous wreck; did you not see his hands shaking? And it took him a while to realise that his glasses were on top of his head all the time." Peigi was more sympathetic.

"I'm surprised to see that young tearaway Donna properly dressed for once. She's never out of these soldiers' trouser things she wears."

"Maybe she's thinking of joining the army," Peigi suggested mischievously, unaccustomed to the wine she had enjoyed for the toasts.

"The best man's making heavy weather of it with her. I hear he was on the rigs with Duncan a while back."

"He's from Fraserburgh if I remember right," responded her sister. "The lassie will be finding him hard to understand. I hardly made out half of his speech; I thought he would never sit down. I don't believe it; look over there Peigi, the MacAskill's daughter Eilidh is with them – and the wee boy Oliver, the poor soul. It's just last year the father and the other brother drowned on Loch Achill. I've heard it said the husband was a bit of a bully. Eilidh sold the fancy house in England and moved back home."

Peigi did not like to speak ill of the dead, she simply nodded in assent. "Who's that in the Strip the Willow with thon slow laddie of the Frasers, the one Johan had when she was well past it?" she asked.

"That's Marianne Morrison," grunted Dollag. "She's a big shot in one of these hospitals where doctors get learned; don't you remember the scandal when she came home with another woman? They'd all expected a man. That's her over yonder in the green trouser suit speaking to the minister's wife."

"I don't see himself." Peigi looked round the room. "He doesn't dance and he's not likely to be in the bar. It can't be much fun being a minister."

Dollag scowled. "Ministers aren't supposed to have fun. He'll be where he should be, at home in his study going over Sunday's sermon. And why is she still here I'd like to know. That's three times I've seen her up dancing with that Kenny Grant."

"But he's lived next door for years; his sister Annie and Chrisanne are great pals." Peigi thought it would be nice to dance with someone as good looking as Kenny Grant. She only got asked up by old nuisances like John MacAngus whose life-long quest to find a wife was a source of much local amusement.

"Kenny seems to be having a long talk with young Norrie Fraser. What do you think that's all about?" Dollag concentrated hard, willing herself to be able to lip read.

"Probably that tractor of his wants sorting again. It's as old as the hills." Peigi wasn't really interested.

"It's Duggie he should be at then. He's the mechanic," Dollag snapped. She'd spotted Bella Nandag doing the Boston Twostep with a strange man. "Who has she got in tow with this time?" she muttered. "There'll be another wee one on the way, mark my words. Has she never heard of counterception?"

MacSweens' General Stores had stoutly resisted stocking the very items which might have prevented such predicaments as the easy-going Bella had found herself more than once. Her oldest, Whitney, was almost twelve.

There was a scuffle in front of the swing doors and the two women saw Neilly Murray, much the worse for drink, being assisted off the premises by Jimmy the Post and Donnie Campbell, himself unusually sober as his bus had been commissioned to return the guests to their homes at a respectable time.

Dollag glanced at her watch. "It's after ten," she announced. "Time we were making tracks."

Peigi knew better than to argue. They collected their jackets from the cloakroom and stepped outside into the cool summer twilight. The moon was almost full and the lively sound of the band followed them along the road.

'Step we gaily on we go, heel for heel and toe . . .'

"What do you think you're doing woman?" Dollag said crossly. Such frivolity was frowned upon. "Get into the side of the road, there's a car coming."

The vehicle approached, slowed and stopped. It was one of these hire drives. A window slid down.

"Could you please tell me where I can find the village hall?" a woman's voice enquired.

"Yes of course," Dollag was quick to oblige. "That's it over there with all the lights. You can't miss it. A young couple got married today . . ."

"Thank you so much. It's been a long time," was the brief reply as the window closed. The sisters watched the car's departure with unconcealed curiosity.

"Who could that be at this time of night?" Peigi wondered. "They'll have a job finding a B&B this late."

"I think," said Dollag, quietly confident, "that perhaps Willie John Morrison is just in for a bit of a surprise!"

Only Half Way

'It's time for some straight talking,' Kenny told his reflection in the steamed-up bathroom mirror. He winced as the spray from the aerosol hit his body. If the advert was to be believed this was the stuff that had girls running after you with unbridled passion. Not exactly how he could describe the person he had admired hopelessly for as long as he could recall. A mature woman, not some flighty girl.

An already married woman, he reminded himself, although from what he had heard there was a distinct coolness in this relationship ever since an incident where she had opted – foolishly perhaps – to 'stray beyond the perceived bounds of convention and respectability.' Her very own words spoken when she had sat in their kitchen with himself and his sister Annie, friend and confidante for many years.

Had the recent more frequent visits been all for Annie's company or did he get the growing feeling that perhaps she hoped to see him as well. It was a thought he at one time would have not dared to entertain but he was becoming more convinced that there were signs. He was also pretty sure his sister knew the score. Last week she had said, 'Kenny will make you a drop of tea, Chrisanne, I'm away out to the henhouse. There's a broody hen ready to sit on some eggs. I'll show you my wedding outfit when I get back."

After several years of 'on and off' Duncan Morrison and Mairi Ross were finally ready to tie the knot and today's celebration had been eagerly anticipated throughout the entire village. Those not at the sit down meal would be expected at the dance afterwards with Roddy William and the Blackhouse Ceilidh Band providing the music. The recently modernised Village Hall had been given as careful a make-over as though 'Hello' magazine's cameramen were out in force instead of Rupert Bingham from the craft shop with his familiar Nikon.

In the time honoured fashion the young couple were first on the floor to the strains of 'Ho ro my nut brown maiden', Duncan a bit red in the face as he beckoned to others to join them. Not much encouragement was needed and as soon as the final slow chord played for the waltz the band swung into the less sedate Dashing White Sergeant which guaranteed a full floor. Anyone left sitting clapped the rhythm. It was going to be great night with the band in top form.

Annie was out in the lobby when the minister came to collect his coat and hat from the cloakroom.

"You're not going away so soon?" she enquired out of politeness, knowing full well that the Reverend MacIntyre was not inclined towards dancing or merrymaking, not even at eight o'clock on a harmless Friday. "Are you not waiting for Chrisanne?"

"Apparently she is not ready to come home." He buttoned up his black coat firmly as though it was November and not a pleasant July evening. Through the glass doors they could see Chrisanne up for a Boston Two Step with old Johnny MacAngus whose unceasing quest for female companionship was renowned in the village.

"Don't worry. We'll get her back with us on the bus, Donnie Campbell's been chartered to lay on transport. Poor soul, he's not had a drop all night."

"He'll be all the better for that," said the minister stiffly as he settled the black hat on his head. "And she can please herself. I'll bid you good night."

His own car was waiting in its customary spot, by unwritten agreement 'The Minister's Parking Place.'

"You know everyone's looking at us," Chrisanne said as Kenny held on to her for the third dance in a row. "Dollag MacSween's got a face on her that would scare the cat."

"I wouldn't let that bother you." Kenny pulled her a little closer as the band drifted into a Gaelic waltz. 'Cailin mo Rúin sa . . .' everyone was singing along to the popular tune. "I've told you how I feel about you. Heaven knows it's taken me long enough to raise the courage. And I'm pretty certain it's not all one sided."

Chrisanne's face turned bright pink. "Oh don't be too sure of that; I am a married woman after all."

"But are you happy?" Her silence was his answer.

"Take your partners for an Eightsome Reel," Roddy William called out.

Kenny let go of her hand. "I want another word with young Norrie Fraser. I'll catch up with you later; you'll come home on the bus with us, won't you? You can sit with Annie and I'll pretend I don't know you." He grinned.

The father of the bride claimed Chrisanne for the Reel.

"You look well in the kilt Eachainn," she said conversationally as they joined hands for the start.

In the middle of this riotous dance a commotion got up just inside the double doors. Chrisanne was in the centre of the circle. 'It'll be Neilly Murray,' she thought. He'd been chucked out earlier on. With a dram in him Neilly was ever ready for a scrap. She wondered how soon she could decently take the floor with Kenny again. At least the MacSween sisters had gone. At the end of the reel the dancers bowed to their partners and thanked them for the pleasure. Red faced and perspiring, Eachain Ross led Chrisanne courteously back to the table where she had sat earlier.

Duncan and his father were seated at the remains of top table. The older man seemed quite agitated, mopping his face with a white hanky. A strange woman had joined them and two young children stared round about in amazement. Annie picked her way back to join Chrisanne.

"What a turn up!" she said excitedly. "That's only Duncan's other sister Kirsty, out of the blue, all the way from Canada, never a word. I don't see the husband though."

"It will give folk something to talk about," laughed Chrisanne. "Dollag and Peigi will be annoyed that they left too soon."

She pondered quietly that it might take any unwanted attention away from herself and Kenny if anything should happen there. Part of her hoped, part of her dreaded the scandal and shame.

The bus was almost at her road end. Annie had already told the driver to let Chrisanne off with herself.

"That's just fine, if she doesn't mind." Donnie Campbell replied. "There's not much room for turning up at the manse, it'll save me backing down."

Annie yawned exaggeratedly. "My feet are on fire," she muttered. "I'm heading straight for bed. Kenny will walk home with you." She gave her friend a goodnight hug.

"As long as it's only half way," Chrisanne said cautiously.

Kenny put his arm round her shoulder as they followed the moonlit path.

'Right now,' he thought 'half way will do just fine.'

The Year in its Seasons

Spring is slow in coming this year. The first tour bus of the season rolls off the ferry in the last week of March. On board, twenty four senior citizens from the Manchester area are making the most of their reduced-rate trip. Views of the fine stretches of sand where churning breakers thunder in are all but obscured as sleety rain driving sharply off the moor batters against the coach windows. Passengers drowsily listen to the driver's practised commentary.

Hardy lambs in windswept fields dash from the shelter of their mothers' woolly sides, frisking and stumbling, running little races, stopping to shiver the wet from their damp bodies.

In MacSweens General Stores Dollag and Peigi are in the throes of a spring clean, routing out cobwebs and the decayed remains of blue-bottles, wiping shelves and rearranging stock. Tins of shortbread left over from last year are on a 'Special Offer' display, a piper playing silently on each lid. A new blue roller blind is installed in the shop window and the chimney sweep booked for Friday.

Buds on the branches of the lonely tree on the moor are reluctant to unfurl. An eerie wind wails through its bare limbs.

Sky and sea vie with one another for the clearest hue of blueness. On what must be the hottest day of summer Peigi is happy that they got the ice cream-making machine set up that week. It is an infernal nuisance to clean but a good little money maker. For the comfort of their customers they have set outdoors an oil-cloth covered table and some chairs under the shade of a striped awning. Sun cream and midge repellent are in steady demand, the shop so busy that a girl newly left the High School comes in half days.

Everyone has their peats home and stacked. Cows drowse lazily on the machair, half-heartedly swishing tails against the persistent flies. Duncan and Mairi's wedding day is blessed with sunshine. Neilly Murray claims he heard a cuckoo but nobody believes him. He is a known liar.

Sheep pant as they lie under the broad green canopy of the lonely tree on the moor, their need for respite overcoming their instinctive fear of this troubled place.

The glorious autumn bloom of the heather is faded, the bracken turned brown and brittle, the sun scarcely seen through rain-plump clouds trailing tattered hems across a surly sky. Fattened and finished, dozens of saleable sheep bleat uneasily from enclosures. Their fate yet to be decided, the lorry will come early next day.

Dollag revises the order from the newsagent wholesaler, not much call more the year for 'Hello' and 'High Gear' or the big English papers. Peigi searches in the long drawer for jam-pot covers, certain that was where she'd seen them last.

A big turn out for the Sacraments is anticipated, one of the visiting ministers – a returning son of the island – has a reputation as a powerful preacher.

Red, russet and golden yellow, the leaves of the lonely tree on the moor prepare to let go. Equinox gales will soon speed their dying. Already there is a chill in the air.

Winter sets up its early warning system with brisk flurries of snow before December has reached its second week. The ferry has been cancelled three times in the past fortnight. Roddy Dubh butchered a bullock, its divided carcase shared between family deep freezes. Deer have been seen coming down off the hills.

On kitchen tables saved by outspread newspapers, Tilley lamps and storm lanterns are checked and cleaned, a wise precaution against breaks in the electricity supply.

MacSweens Stores gets a delivery from the Calor Gas truck, its driver gratefully accepting a mug of strong tea on such a cold day. Boxes of old fashioned candles and a selection of torch batteries are on a rack next to the till. Christmas stock fills prominent places on the shelves – plastic holly and reindeer horns and wooden instructions for Santa to stop. Decorations and cards, the January page in the 2008 calendar a sparkling scene of frozen lochs and a quotation from Ecclesiastes.

Children are on a countdown to parties and presents. Dollag frowns, fearing correctly that the true meaning of the Christian festival has somehow been diminished.

The lonely tree on the moor keeps constant watch, its lichened limbs a reminder of the innocent who had once come to them to end his tormented life, hanging and dying as the curlew's cry carried away his soul.

Vacancy

Shaded light from his reading lamp revealed tight-lipped concentration. It was important to get the wording right, with no misleading messages, no suggestions of levity. Further procrastination was not an option; it was time to admit he needed practical help. Angry independence and the well-intentioned support of some ladies in his congregation served no long term solution. It was almost a year since his wife had left. There was positively no hope of a reconciliation and now, the spectre of divorce hung over him. No blame laid at his door it was to be understood.

'Housekeeper wanted for Manse in Island Village. Full time position. Mature person preferred.' Would that be a suitable opening? Composing a sermon was never so demanding. The embarrassing subject of remuneration would have to be dealt with, perhaps best use the term 'fair' for the moment, specifics could be gone into later provided there were any responses.

'No children or other encumbrances . . .' Were you permitted to make such stipulations in these days of political correctness? And where to place the advertisement? Certainly not in the local newspaper; only a total stranger would be appropriate for this situation. It was probably better to contact a Daily from Glasgow or Aberdeen.

Searching for an envelope, Reverend MacIntyre considered it probable that one got what one deserved in life rather than what one hoped for. As a young man he had cherished ambitions to work in the media perhaps as a journalist or broadcaster. A determined father had other ideas, pushing him firmly in the direction of the Church. His older brothers had done nothing to distinguish themselves professionally, preferring more lucrative work on North Sea rigs.

In the happier early days Chrisanne, fresh faced and innocent, had welcomed his tentative overtures. They had met on a 'Significant Scripture' course in a picturesque village near Edinburgh, he, recently ordained, a voluntary tutor, she a confused youngster who he found out much later had been sent there by strict parents following an infatuation with an older man. A shared enjoyment of the countryside led to pleasant times in each other's company and relaxing evenings were spent with others in the study group after

Devotions were over for the day. Both were good singers in the traditional style.

Her family was more than encouraging. He suspected correctly that they saw a minister as quite a 'catch' which would give their social standing in the community a tremendous boost. Almost resigned to bachelordom he was approaching forty years of age and Chrisanne had just turned twenty three on the day Archie MacDougall, college friend and fellow minister, had pronounced them man and wife in his own familiar white-walled church.

Right from the start Chrisanne had tackled her duties as a minister's wife with youthful enthusiasm. The good ladies of the Guild had taken her under their collective wing dispensing encouragement and advice with motherly concern. If she made mistakes they were more than compensated for by her bright personality and genuine desire to help others. The general opinion was that the Reverend MacIntyre had made a wise choice in spite of the discrepancy of ages. Indeed, he considered himself a lucky man.

It was with interest that the village folk awaited signs that the Manse might expect the patter of tiny feet. Chrisanne could not cross the threshold of the General Stores without enduring the close scrutiny of Hector MacSween or one of his nosy daughters. The time came when she began to harbour concerns that something might be amiss. An appointment with a specialist had been arranged to coincide with a visit to her sister in Inverness. Later results proved there to be no impediments. The gynaecologist had suggested that she ask her husband to undertake similar investigation. This provoked the most bitter row. It flew in the face of the Will of the Almighty, the outraged minister declared. The matter was not to be referred to again. Chrisanne bore her disappointment without complaint and continued in her efforts to support the Young Wives and Toddlers who had established a playgroup in the Church Hall. Without the support of Annie, her neighbour and friend, she would have at times found it hard to maintain a pretence that all was well with her world.

Oblivious to her distress the Reverend MacIntyre went about his religious duties in an unchanging way although the same could not be said for his matrimonial ones. That sort of thing was for younger folk, he excused himself, and if Chrisanne was concerned by his lack of attention she neither said nor did anything about it.

Matters came unexpectedly to an explosive head some years later on the day his wife went to town leaving home like the proverbial country mouse and returning late in the afternoon in the guise of a painted trollop. The minister still shuddered when recalling his extreme reaction following a tiring and frustrating day; how he had seen it as a challenge to his authority and had thumped the table and called her despicable names; how she had subsequently fled for reassurance to the house of their neighbour. Pride and hurt feelings at the time had kept him from begging forgiveness and the atmosphere between them had not surprisingly been strained.

The missive now signed and sealed, Reverend MacIntyre laid it on the hall table to be posted the following day. Catching sight of himself in the small mirror – the face creased, the jowls saggy, the fair hair all but gone he thought bleakly that it was little wonder that Chrisanne should have sought solace elsewhere with a younger attractive man. He had it on the good authority of a venerable matron of the parish that a pram would shortly sit outside a certain farm cottage in rural Aberdeenshire. Blinking heavily, he offered up a kindly prayer that all would be well; older mothers often had greater difficulties to face.

The clock chimed ten. Time for the TV News, he thought, a cup of cocoa and then upstairs to a lonely bed.

Going to Town

"You're surely not going over dressed like that." Ishbel tugged her friend's sleeve.

"It might be cold on the boat," said Mina, determinedly buttoning up her good navy blue coat. "Even if it is July; you never can tell."

"Have you nothing lighter, like a fleece?" Ishbel's was green, with a hood.

"The only fleece here is on the sheep," retorted Mina, a resolute resister of change.

"Come on then, Flag is outside with the car. We need to be at the pier sharp."

The two women climbed in, reaching for seat belts and enquiring after the health of the driver as was the custom.

"You'll get a good crossing; there's no word of a wind." Flag said conversationally. "Are you going for a bit of shopping?"

"Just there and back. We'll have to look lively. I think we get about three hours in Inverness. I'm after a few bits and pieces but Mina here is looking for . . ."

Mina's elbow dug sharply into Ishbel's side. "He doesn't want to know all the details," she hissed.

"We should be home in time to catch Donnie's bus on the way back," Ishbel told Flag as they parked near the terminal, "but if not we'll give you a shout if that's all right."

They waved him off and joined the short queue for tickets.

"He's a nice looking lad your nephew," observed Mina as they filled in their boarding passes. "Is he still going out with that girl from Carloway?"

"Oh indeed, he is that," said Ishbel. "We can likely expect wedding bells in the autumn next year. A grand excuse for another shopping trip to Inverness."

"If I get an invite." Mina sniffed, gripping the stout handles of the brown holdall she insisted on taking everywhere.

"And what about your own nephew?" Ishbel enquired. "We thought he hit it off rather well with that girl his sister brought home. You know, when their Mam had her seventieth."

"Oh the *foreign* one with the bracelets." Mina had not been impressed. "Aye, he seems quite keen. He's never off the phone and he clipes to her on that computer thing."

Nothing more was said as they climbed the long covered walkway to where the 'Isle of Lewis' was tied up. Others were boarding, strangers mostly – holiday people dragging wheeled cases, younger folk laden with monstrously cumbersome rucksacks, their bare brown legs sticking out from colourful shorts and ending in chunky hiking boots. A group of five carried musical instruments in black cases. Mina gave them a glare as if daring them to create a disturbance on the way.

On board, the ladies settled themselves into seats in the observation lounge. All around, fellow travellers clearly unused to such an early start were arranging themselves and their belongings with subdued voices and half-hidden yawns. A child cried and someone's mobile phone trilled a tiresome tune. "I'm on the ferry," the recipient was heard to say.

"I'll get us something to read once the shop opens," said Ishbel. The commotion of departure commenced – raised voices, clanging of metal, sudden acceleration of the powerful engines as the vessel drew away from its berth. Moments later the tannoy crackled into life and a man's voice welcomed them on board on behalf of the ferry company. He spoke in English and in Gaelic, explaining details of procedures for emergency abandonment of the ship, where to find life jackets and places to assemble should the need arise.

"Did you hear what he said?" Mina shifted uneasily in her seat. "I don't like the sound of that, going on about lifejackets and things, they must think something is going to go wrong."

Ishbel smiled. "I'm quite sure it won't; it's just stuff they have to say nowadays for health and safety. There will be nothing to worry about. Do you want a Peoples Friend?" She rose from her seat fumbling her purse out of her handbag.

As it made its solitary progress through the unpredictable vastness of the Minch the boat ran into a heavy swell. Sea-spray sliced across the curved glass of the seating area as the bows dipped and rose, the engines' notes changing whenever the props lost their forward thrust.

"I've never liked this bit," muttered Mina, folding her magazine firmly into the brown bag and fastening the zip with a flourish as if anticipating an immediate departure.

Ishbel patted her arm reassuringly. "It's fine. I've seen it much worse. We can go to the restaurant in a wee while for a bite of breakfast. It will be calmer once we get near land."

There was a shorter distance to walk on the Ullapool side where buses waited for passengers to board. Unencumbered by luggage Ishbel and Mina found a seat near the front. Their coach eased its way into the stream of assorted vehicles which had driven over the dropped ramp and up the slipway. Soon the village was left behind. As the road climbed steeply toward Braemore Junction the bus was forced to slow down, held back by a huge lorry-mounted crane crawling in the whine of a low gear. People were half-rising in their seats trying to see what was the problem.

"That's all we need," said Mina. "Haven't we little enough time in the town?"

"I saw that thing coming off the boat well in front of us," replied Ishbel, "and I wondered if we would catch up with it. He's gone into the lay-by. It will be a slow journey for him wherever he's going."

There was a collective sigh of relief as the bus trundled past, its driver sounding his horn in grateful acknowledgement.

"What are you up for in the town?" Mina enquired, accepting a fruit pastille.

"I'm after a cardigan for myself and a nightdress for Granny MacIver and I might get something for Bella Nandag's new baby. She's got another wee girl."

"You're surely not buying something for that trollop?" Mina spoke disapprovingly. "Who's the father this time?"

"Och she's not all that bad, just a bit easily led. Her mother and my cousin Billy John are related on the MacDonald side. She was very good to our old grandfather when his legs went bad on him. She'd go out to the van for his messages and bring him a Gazette on a Thursday if she was in town. He liked a kipper as well."

"Oh well then." Mina was not convinced.

Heads nodded drowsily as the summer-green countryside sped past. Remarks were passed on the expanding sprawl of the city as

96

they eventually crossed the Kessock Bridge. The bus thudded over the speed bumps and pulled up at the roundabout.

"Right," said Ishbel as they climbed down at the bus stance. "It's quicker to the shops if we cut through the train station."

In Falcon Square some kind of open air festival was in progress. There was lively music and the unmistakeable smell of fast food frying. The shopping mall was thronged and the ladies took a moment to get their bearings.

"Would you look at some of these styles!" Mina exclaimed in horror as they glanced at window models draped in flimsy items which gave maximum exposure to indecent amounts of flesh.

"You'd be a sensation at a wedding in an outfit like that," Ishbel said jokingly.

"Be quiet with you. I'd catch my death of cold." Mina glowered. They walked on through the jostling crowd,

"That was a waste of time," grumbled Mina later as they walked out of Debenhams and into the heat of the arcade. "Nothing at all there I liked." She fanned her face. "It's so warm. I could do with a cup of tea."

"Didn't I say the coat was too much? You could at least open the buttons. The tea will have to wait; let's get you sorted out first. We'll try Marks&Spencer."

Ishbel checked her watch. "It's going on for twelve," she said as they went in. "If you go over there where these two girls are putting frocks back onto hangers you can tell them what you want and they'll help you choose. I'm going to nip downstairs and get a jumper or maybe a shirt for Flag. It was good of him to pick us up for the boat. The baby clothes are on that floor too. I won't need long to get the rest of what's on my list. Will you be OK on your own?"

"Of course I will," insisted Mina, firmly clutching the brown holdall. You could never be sure. Her purse was in it with all of last week's pension and the £25 gift token that her niece had sent.

"Can we help you?" came the pleasant enquiry as Mina approached the busy girls.

"I'm looking for a costume," she stated. The girls exchanged looks. They were very young.

"A costume? Is it for a party?" enquired the one called Madeline.

"No, it's for a wedding; something in a nice grey or maybe a light brown. And not too short in the skirt."

"Ah, you mean a suit, a two-piece? Yes, I'm sure we can find you something. Would you like to come with me?" Madeline led the way.

Half an hour later Ishbel spotted a disgruntled looking Mina leaving the 'pay-here' counter.

"Well then, did you get what you were wanting?" she asked, her own satisfactory purchases enclosed in the store's distinctive carrier bags.

"I never in my life saw the like! Jackets with no collars and just one button to fasten them. Skirts with hems that went up one minute and down the next – and as for the colours! I don't want to stand out like a red MacBraynes funnel or a banana on legs. I'll need to take another look through J.D.'s catalogue when we get home."

"I see you must have bought something." Ishbel pointed to the carrier bag being stowed into the holdall.

"Yes, yes, I spent my Christmas token on a blouse, a pale blue, buttons right up to the neck, nice plain cuffs. It will be fine with what I wear to church."

"Have you tried it on?" asked Ishbel. "It's a long way to come back if you need to exchange it."

Mina shook her head.

"Come on then; we've still got a minute. I'll keep your coat for you, and the holdall if you like. What else is this you bought?" She noticed a smaller bag.

"What do you think?" Mina mumbled, turning slightly pink in the face. "What do all the best people come to this shop for? I'll show you." She revealed a bargain pack of six full-fit knickers in size 18.

"Are they not lovely?" She beamed. "Pastel shades."

"They'll fairly brighten up your washing line," Ishbel was amused.

"What do you mean washing line? Do you think I would hang my unmentionables on view for every passing eye?" Mina was outraged. "They'll be just fine on the pulley in my kitchen."

Time for a Change

It was when I was coming home the other night I decided that this has got to stop. I was not getting any younger and I'd put on a bit of weight. There had been plenty of knock-backs over the years but I had always kept hoping that my luck might change one of these fine days.

There was a time when I'd have pedalled all the way up Cnoc Ard but now I'm off the bicycle half way up and scarcely a breath left for a draw on my fag. It would have taken then but two little hops and swing the leg over, cranking that bit harder to get a peep of light from the wee front lamp but nowadays I'm having to sit astride like a woman before there's enough go in me to get a start.

I remember too how I would have slung a bag of peat or a sick sheep across the handlebars and thought nothing of it. Aye, and many the lassie going home after the dance was pleased to take a perch on my cross-bar, the smell of her scent and the sweat from the eightsome sweet in my face as I held her steady and enjoyed to hear her laugh with maybe the promise of a bit of a kiss behind the stack before she went to her door. And keeping an eye out for the cailleach who never seemed to sleep.

There was the two sisters, Mairi and Seonag. Och it seemed the decent thing to give them both a turn. The fuss they made, you'd have thought some dreadful crime had been committed.

I'm in my old brown chair now with the fire stirred to life and a drop of whisky to relax the weary bones.

'John MacAngus, bachelor of this parish,' I say out loud, startling the collie. 'Where did you go so wrong so many times over the years?' Well, it wasn't for want of trying. There was a while Annie Gillies seemed keen enough but she went off to the nursing. Then after that two English women came into Ian Willie's place, Lavender and Beryl if I mind right, daft names like you'd expect from the Sassanach. I tried being friendly, stopping at the gate when they were out in front with the hens thinking they'd ask me in for a wee cup of tea. Strange looks was all I got. Then I was over offering to lend a hand with fixing the fence but they'd have none of it, did not want to feel 'obliged' I think was the word, no understanding at all of the ways of Highland folk. A man came from the town with his name painted on the side of a yellow van, he likely charged them the earth.

It's not that I have nothing to offer a reasonable woman; I'm all alone in the house since I lost my mother nineteen years ago. The two of us managed fine as far back as I remember without bothering with the like of central heating – nothing wrong with a good peat fire – and she never minded the old cracked sink in the kitchen. I don't even get in the way that much. I mend the shoes in the wee shed round the back of the scullery. That's why they call me 'Johnny Brógan'.

You'd expect the garden to be women's work of course, gives them a chance to do their own thing as they say. A few rolls of wire netting and the sheets of corrugated iron that blew off the byre roof wouldn't be all that hard to shift. Johan Matheson would have been just right for the job; you should have seen the arms on her. She was broad in the stern as well. After she married Norrie from the garage the pram was never empty. Mind you, I'm not all that keen on children. They'd be wanting computers and fancy clothes and holidays on the mainland. And I would have had to paper the upstair rooms as well. Och I'm far better off without any of that.

It's a mystery to me why I seem to have ended up on my own. Old Willie John Morrison used to tell me to go up to town and get my teeth fixed but only the Good Lord knows how much that would have set me back. I'm not too fussy if the women are young or wearing on a bit, you'd think there would be someone out there with a notion for a fine looking man with a good set of whiskers and a cow calving every year. This east coast woman called Maggie came to keep house for the minister after his wife left …Well, if *herself* was just wanting a wee change I'd have been more than willing to take her on. And then this bold Maggie had high hopes of marrying the minister and him a bodach older than Methusalah.

Bella Shaw, a niece of Sandy Dolan's, came home to settle after years of working in a shop in Kyle of Lochalsh. I asked her to the dancing a couple of times and we went all the way to Rodel in John Maclennan's minibus when he did the tourist runs in the summer. She was getting keen enough. They said she was a great cook and not afraid of a bit of hard work about the place. Then one afternoon when I went over with the boots I'd mended for Sandy she was in the kitchen looking through JD Williams catalogue for something to wear for the 'going-away' and not a word had I spoken about marriage. When I took another look at her I had the feeling that I would not want to waken up with that face on the pillow next to me so I told her as politely as I could that I was suddenly called away to look after a sick aunt over in the Black Isle and had no idea when I'd be back.

It was after I came home from there at the end of October I started to realise I wasn't as fit as I once was. More than one bicycle had served me well over the years but I was finding it harder to get about particularly as I seemed to have further and further to go if I was to find the right woman. So tonight I have made up my mind to write a wee letter to that man over in Aberdeenshire that comes across with the hay and ask him if he'll get me some kind of second-hand tractor; then by Jove who knows, on a good day I might get as far as Garynahine.

Oh there's life in this old dog yet . . .

Fireside Memories

"Roddy Matheson, you rascal, we were beginning to think you were never coming home," Katie Mary piled up the empty plates. "How long now since you've been away from here? You were never much of a letter writer."

"It's a good twenty years I expect. Time just runs away from you when it's all so different from what you've grown up with," said her brother. "It took me long enough to make up my mind. I always hoped . . ."

"Well, you did the right thing. Growing up with three bossy big sisters couldn't have been easy! Not that there was much work here anyway. You had such lovely thick dark hair." Katie Mary had a photo in her hand. "Rhoda took this the day before you sailed."

"That was the style in those days," Roddy said, patting his head. "Not much left there now! It's yourself hasn't changed a bit; has she Donald?" He turned to his brother-in-law with a smile.

"Well, I don't know about that." Donald MacLeod heaved himself up from his chair and reached into the press for the bottle of fine Islay Malt bought specially for the wanderer's return. "She has certainly kept me in my place all these years even if we didn't always agree ... but I don't think I could have managed without her."

"Get away with you," Katie Mary called from the doorway. "No need for that soft soaping. It's fine I know the two of you will sit with that bottle till all hours so I'm away over to Murdina's. I might stay the night; their youngest is teething and Granny could make herself useful." She pushed the door shut with her foot.

"You will see a lot of change here since you left." Donald poured two generous measures. "The new Community Hall for a start. Do you mind the old ramshackle place it used to be? Rusty corrugated iron and hardly room to breathe when a dance was on. There was a lottery grant and a lot of local support. You'll not have known Aggie Bell who cleans the school? Well, she was the power behind a lot of the work that was done."

"I mind well the great nights we had there in our young days." Roddy's voice was tinged with the nostalgic recollection of the returning son. "Always someone to play for the dancing, the women ready with tea and a bite to eat – didn't they make stovies? And us lot out round the back with the half bottles and maybe a fight getting up. One against one. It was all good crack, not like today's pitched battles."

"We never thought how worried our mothers were. My own one, God rest her, she'd not go to bed till Bobban and myself were home."

The peats settled in the fire and Donald reached to the wicker basket for more.

"Did you never think of getting a wife all these years in Detroit City? There must have been plenty lassies to choose from."

"Och I was aye that bit shy you know, not much of a social mixer. I had plenty other things to keep me busy. There was always someone needing a motor fixed. I used to fish a lot, kept a boat on the Lakeside harbour. Did I never tell you? I did quite a bit of climbing as well. A group of us guys used to charter a small plane and head for Missouri or Kentucky. After a week in the factory the outdoors was a welcome relief. There was only one girl for me back home but I was too bashful to make a move."

"Don't think your sister and myself didn't guess about Annie Gillies. We thought you might have come home for her father's funeral. Poor Callum, a sad lonely death on the shore. The croft is empty just now; the last tenants couldn't handle the winter weather. If you are ever thinking of settling back here that would be a grand place, nice sheltered cove for your boat and all. You never know how things might work out."

"It's a bit late for all that." Roddy paused. "I'm thinking it will only be the bachelor life for me though I do envy you and Katie Mary and your fine family."

"Speaking of bachelors," Donald broke in. "Do you remember John MacAngus, the shoemaker?"

"Oh aye, him they called Johnny Brógan," said Roddy. "He was always after the girls. Did he ever get lucky?"

"Not yet, but not for want of trying. He's a bit of a legend," Donald reflected. "For a couple of years he courted Mairi Malcolm from the Caley Hotel. We thought they would make a go of it. Then she found out he was seeing her sister Seonag on the quiet. There was a big bust up. Mairi Malcolm married a man from Buckie, a fish salesman. She hasn't been home here since they moved east. Seonag got a fine lad from the town. They have a shop in Firth Street, Hi Fi's and television sets. That's where we got our last one."

The large TV watched silently from its wooden cabinet as Roddy held out his empty glass. "Yes thanks," he hinted. "I'll manage another wee dram. That one went down a treat."

Donald leaned over with the bottle. "And there's more. There was never a sign of MacAngus settling. You'd see him pedalling out the peat road on an old bicycle. He hung about MacSweens' Stores quite a bit with a notion for Peigi. Her sister would have none of it. Then he went after a couple of daft English women – they bought Ian Willie's old croft. Neither of them took him on. They had goats and bantam hens and some Shetland ponies – fairly fancied themselves fit for Island life."

Donald laughed at the recollection of them in their tartan skirts and serviceable wellingtons trying to chase the hens into their shed, the one lot cackling as loud as the other.

"But I'll give them their due. Before they left there was a very kind sum of money donated to the new Hall project. We were quite sorry to see them go. The teacher's husband's daughter still has the pony they left her."

"The teacher. Surely not thon fearful Miss Mason!"

"No, no. She left long ago – 1996 I think. The new young teacher's from Skye. She married Jacob MacDonald from Linga Farm. His first wife died young."

The red glow from the fire and the satisfying sensation of the whisky going down was putting a comfortable warmth right through Roddy. It was good to be back among his own people. "And did the Brógan give up after that?"

"No nor give up." Donald thought for a moment. "It could have been Sheila Mackay that was next. He even tried for Maggie Jessop who was keeping house for the minister. No luck there at all. The minister kept too close an eye on her. Well, there was Janet MacGregor who worked in a bank in the town, a right bonnie lassie. He was old enough to be her father. It wasn't long before she got a lad her own age, a son of Calum the plumber."

Donald screwed up his face, searching for memories.

"And there was a lassie who worked on the ferry, from Oban I think, but she took to the drink and that was the end of another romance. And Sandy Dolan's niece. She had a face like a donkey. She was keen enough but Johnny took cold feet – it was getting too serious too quickly. She started looking for going away outfits but it was Brógan who went away. He stayed on the mainland for a few months at his auntie's.

"That old bicycle must have covered a lot of miles," Roddy remarked. "Is it still on the road?"

"Bicycle?" Donald was smiling now. "He must have worn out two or three bicycles over the years. But if you keep a look out tomorrow about ten past six you'll see him heading off on his latest crusade. The bike's no use to him these days but the crafty old devil never gives up. He bought an old Nuffield tractor from that man down Banff way who brings over the hay and straw. There's nobody left within cycling distance."

"I always thought she was not cut out to be a minister's wife." Dollag put the packs of bacon into their allocated space in the chill cabinet.

"Do you remember that bright green jacket she used to wear to church? Not the proper thing at all."

"Aye I do that," responded her sister Peigi, clicking her teeth disapprovingly as she studied the sell-by dates on Tuesday's loaf and hoped they'd not have to reduce the price. "And her often without a hat on."

"Don't forget the time she went to town and came back dressed like a fashion model." Dollag warmed to her critical theme. "There was the smell of perfume in the bus for days after, Donnie Campbell told me, and he heard that . . ."

The shop bell pinged and quivered on its curved metal arm as the door opened. A woman wearing a navy gabardine coat and a checked headscarf walked into the silence which had fallen. Two pairs of inquisitive eyes followed her short passage to the counter.

"Good afternoon to you Miss Jessop. What can we be getting for you today?" Attempting what she hoped was a sympathetic smile, Dollag wiped her hands on her overall. "Something nice for poor Reverend MacIntyre's tea perhaps?"

"Are you needing bread at all?" Peigi chimed in. "This one's grand for toast."

"And how is the dear man?" Dollag enquired. "We all know what a terrible shock it was to him, Chrisanne eh …leaving like that."

Maggie Jessop produced her purse and forced a smile. She'd met their like many times before and was expert at avoiding careless disclosures which would be passed on with the typical exaggeration of those who have the ear of many eager listeners.

"Everything is just fine ladies," she ventured. "I am only needing a tin of Ovaltine and some digestive biscuits if you have them."

Dollag reached to the shelf. "Och the poor soul," she said. "Not finding it easy to sleep then is he? Well, I'm not surprised. They say lavender is very helpful. We have some soap and bath-oil if he'd like to give it a try. Will that be all for now?" She took the proffered note and meticulously counted back the change ever hopeful of some last minute confidence.

As the Manse housekeeper swept out a second customer appeared. Dollag sniffed with disappointment. There would be nothing newsworthy forthcoming here. Annie Grant, sister of the conniving man who had notoriously made off with the minister's wife, had already made it publicly clear that she neither condemned nor approved what had taken place. It was nobody else's business; she did not intend to let it alter her own life in any way. Her brother had put young Norrie Fraser from the garage in charge of the croft work. He was a willing worker with little hope of a place of his own. Norrie Senior had always been aware of his son's keenness to work on the land and the family business was well enough secured by having his second son Duggie and his twin sister Evie as competent mechanics. Between them they also ran breakdown recovery and taxi services.

"Well, she's not got much to say for herself," muttered Peigi after Annie left the shop with her sausages and a bag of sugar. "On the shelf now without a doubt. I've never heard of any man looking the way of her."

"Not even John MacAngus, the bachelor, and he had a try at near everyone in the place, including yourself." Dollag laughed, prodding her sister teasingly. "I mind how he used to come in for his tobacco and he'd be whistling 'Peigi a'ghráidh' and your face would go bright pink."

"I don't remember anything of the kind," Peigi protested, colouring slightly at the embarrassing recollection. "That one was never the sort for settling down; pity help the poor woman who'd have been foolish enough to take him on."

"Well, he never gives up even though he's as old as the hills. I see he's got a tractor now; the bike's too much for him." Dollag shook her head. "It will be the finish of him. You wait and see. Watch out, here comes that rascal of Bella Nandag's, the one they call Terry. He's with Robbie from the craft shop . . . and Don-Alec McAskill's wee grandson, we don't see *him* very often."

"Hallo boys, is that you home from school then? Will it be crisps you're after?" They lived too close to the school to qualify for the bus though Donnie Diesel never went by them on wilder winter days.

Dollag kept a wary eye on the young customers as they made their selection.

"Oliver's paying," said the biggest boy as they laid their packets on the counter.

"Thank you very much." Oliver smiled as Dollag counted back his change. The likeness to Don-Alec was there all right she thought, and wasn't it nice to see a boy with such good manners?

"Tell your Granda and Granny we were asking for them. I haven't seen them in a while." Dollag knew fine they went to town for most of their shopping.

The two women stood quietly for a moment after the boys left then Peigi spoke. "There's something about that boy. It makes me uneasy thinking about it. He might be more like his grandfather than just his looks."

"What are you on about now? You've too much imagination – that's your trouble." snapped Dollag

"Well, I hope you're right," came the subdued reply. "I can't help but remember about Don-Alec and the time he saw the lights on the hillside. People said they were a warning that something terrible was about to happen."

"Do you mean to tell me you believe all that ancient tales?" Dollag was not so easy to convince. "Oh aye, I know it was just about the time when old Calum Gillies collapsed on the shore. There was a storm and a boat had come in on the rocks. The lights had nothing to do with it."

"Plenty folk round this way think differently." Peigi believed the old superstitions implicitly. There was no point going on about it, Dollag always got the better of her younger sister when it came to an argument.

"Put up the closed sign. I'm pulling down the blind." Dollag's voice was gentler than usual. "It's about time for some supper – there's a couple of chops in the fridge. We'll have them with a new potato."

Peigi checked that all was properly secure. You were never sure in this day and age though not many years back locked doors were unheard of. She picked up the loaf she knew would be out of date by morning.

"I could make a bread and butter pudding for afters," she suggested, lifting the counter flap.

"Did you hear about Mairead Ben Uilleam?" she heard Dollag call from the scullery. "Jimmy the Post told me. It seems she had ..."

The rest of the sentence was drowned out by the sound of the kettle being filled at the tap. There was no doubt, thought Peigi, that she would hear more later.

Taking the risk

"I'll think about it," Oliver's mother had said, buying some time. Her son had asked if he could join his two pals on an overnight camp-out in the now disused shieling on the other side of Tor Chamais. It wasn't trekking in Nepal or crossing the Sahara – surely she was just being over-protective? Oliver was twelve and not much given to reckless behaviour. She knew Robbie Bingham from the craft shop was a sensible lad but Terry Anderson was a bit of a tearaway from a more dubious background.

Having lived for years under the dominance of her overbearing late husband Eilidh often found it difficult to think and decide for herself but after the terrible boating accident she had been in no doubt of the direction she must take. The family solicitor had dealt with financial matters promptly. She needed little persuasion to sell the far too grand house in York and return to the Highland home where her parents still lived. Don-Alec MacAskill, her father, had organised permission for a site to be cleared on his own ground for a bungalow to be built. It would include four or five rooms which Eilidh planned to use for Bed and Breakfast. There was always a huge demand for good accommodation for most of the year. It was something she knew she would enjoy. This enthusiasm was shared by her mother Cathy who liked nothing better than to see shining surfaces and neatly ironed bedcovers.

She named the house 'Ceol na Mara' unashamed of her lack of originality. An attractive website had ensured a lot of interest from the start and this year some of the first guests had returned. Eilidh's early worries about not being able to cope were unfounded; between them she and her mother had the place running like clockwork. She was happy meeting new people and being busy was the best way of occupying her mind though the terrible events of the past could not be totally pushed aside. She was ashamed to realise how little she missed her pompous husband Willerby who had been of the 'little woman's place is in the home with the children' persuasion and any attempts on Eilidh's part to persuade him otherwise had been met with derision. But the loss of Oliver's older brother Harold was as painful now as it had been on the day the young policeman had knocked on their door.

The other two boys had to cycle to Oliver's place. Robbie joked about his bike probably being an old one of Johnny Brógan's. He was the middle child of a family of five and the craft shop was very dependent on a good tourist season. It was hard not to envy Oliver's cracking new multi-geared model until Robbie realised that having his Dad at home was a much better deal. Terry Anderson had never known his father, some amateur football player with whom his easy going mother had had a brief dalliance.

They crested the brow of the hill after a couple of hours and the shieling was vaguely visible through a smirr of rain which had accompanied them for the last leg of the climb. On the downward slope the heather grew thickly.

Oliver said, "What a good job we didn't bring Horace." Horace was his Bassett Hound, a dog which enjoyed a scamper on the beach but was not designed to cope on rough moorland. Crisps and juice and a fat bar of chocolate soon restored their strength before they roamed off to gather brushwood and anything which would later make a fire. Terry's task was to fill the empty plastic container with water from the stream from which the grazing cattle had once drunk on their summer pasture. Further down it tumbled into a cascade. Bits of a broken fence still endured after long years of Highland weather.

"Come here boys, I've found something." They heard Terry yelling. Oliver and Robbie raced over. A rucksack and a pair of walking poles lay in the ragged grass next to the lopsided posts.

"D'you think someone's gone over the edge?" Oliver was concerned. Terry slid forward on his stomach until he could look down. A woman was lying on the ridge below.

"Hey, can you hear me? Are you all right?" he bawled. The figure on the grass stirred and attempted to sit up. She waved an arm feebly.

"Please can you go and get help? I was trying for a good photo and got too near the edge. My leg is rather sore. You'll find a phone in my backpack."

Robbie had a rummage about. He knew his own one was out of credit. There was little chance of a signal up here anyway. Terry had found out that the woman's name was Gina. This was turning into quite an adventure. They sat on a rock discussing and deciding. There was a rope in the bothy. One of them would be lowered down to where Gina lay and then they could hoist her back to the top. Who'd go down? Robbie was terrified of heights. Terry, the oldest, was built like a bull and was just as cumbersome. Oliver was slighter and pretended to be brave so it would need to be him. That was the plan.

Pottering in the kitchen in the late afternoon Oliver's Granny saw the boys on their way back down the hill. Certain that something must have happened she called to her husband and Eilidh who set off at once to meet the returning party. A quick look through the spyglass had shown more than three figures in the huddle. But it looked like someone was hurt.

"Please God, not Oliver – he's all I have left." Eilidh muttered under her breath.

Later the story unfolded as Gina, her foot strapped and her strength revived by a good strong cup of tea, praised the courage of the boys who had come to her aid.

"Especially this lad." She smiled towards Oliver.

"When I saw him coming down on that rope ..." she broke off, recalling the relief.

Eilidh didn't know whether to be proud or angry. Cathy bustled in saying they had nobody booked for Room Three and Gina was to stop for the night, there was to be no arguing. Someone would drive her back to the Hostel in the morning. She'd phoned to let them know Gina was all right.

Oliver's grandfather came in to his room to say good night and to tell Oliver how impressed they were that he'd been such a hero.

"It still was a quite a risk you took, thank God it turned out well," he said gruffly.

"It's OK Grandfather," Oliver confided. "I saw Harold before I went over the slope. He said it was going to be all right. I didn't feel scared after that. You do believe me don't you? But maybe we shouldn't tell the others."

Don-Alec nodded gravely. He'd suspected for some time that this boy was 'different'. Hadn't he seen the omen of 'lights on the hill' the day before his brother drowned?

"Goodnight son, sleep well," he said, closing the door gently.

Giving something back.

It was not a place of happy memories but Gerald felt he should go back. He had thought about it several times as he was growing up. Excuses were easily found – his work, his current fragile relationship, his lack of courage along with apprehension as to how he would be received. Still, he felt he owed it to his parents. The memory of their deaths all these years ago was as fresh today as if he was still on that island shore, the devilish wind shrieking over the wreckage of the boat as he watched the old crofter's valiant attempts to save them. For this the poor man had paid with his own life.

Gerald had been left alone on the shore clinging pitifully to the soaking black fur of a shivering collie dog whose mournful howls were lost in the hail-studded gloom. He had crouched in silence in the lee of a big rock frozen with cold and terror. The sight of Dougal Kennedy the Coastguard's bulky body looming out of the darkness had made his stomach churn with relief. Gulping through tears Gerald tried to tell what had happened. The man had carried him to his parked Landrover wrapping him in a salty smelling blanket while he made urgent calls to the appropriate people. Gerald had wanted to take the dog. The Coastguard said no. He will want just now to watch over his master, but maybe later. He said some words in a strange tongue then in English told him the dog was called Cuillin. Somehow this simple information brought some comfort to the boy. He repeated the name quietly to himself.

The Coastguard's kindly wife Rhoda kept him occupied for the next few days. He helped her feed the hens and went with her to the butcher's van or the village store where there was always a sweetie for him while the women discussed his plight in Gaelic with much sighing and head shaking. The old dog Cuillin had lain on a mat at the foot of his bed at night while Gerald tried not to cry. The reality of his newly orphaned state was hard for an eleven year old boy to deal with. He kept hoping it was a terrible, bad dream from which he would soon wake. He felt sorry too for poor Cuillin who often whimpered as he slept.

As soon as the needful arrangements for the deceased had been made his father's brother came to take him away. He was to live with this uncle and an aunt and two cousins, none of whom he really knew. A forlorn Gerald said goodbye to Rhoda and Dougal and hugged the dog who licked his face sympathetically. He hadn't the courage to ask if his uncle had a dog back in Penrith.

The aunt and uncle had never been close to his parents. Gerald recalled the unpleasant scenes which had accompanied their rare visits. His mother had been difficult to get along with, self willed and determined and much given to screaming tantrums. Taking the 'anything for a quiet life' approach his father had seldom stood up to her demands. Gerald tried to remain as inconspicuous as possible. Shy and withdrawn, he had few friends at school. He studied hard and brought home excellent reports which he timidly presented to his mother in the hope of approval. She gave them the briefest of glances and passed some non-committal remark. Gerald knew she didn't care. His father always tried to reward him in some small and treasured way. When he was a bit taller, Father would say, he'd let him help more with the boat. A new luxury cabin cruiser had been acquired at that Spring's boat show. Mother had had her way as usual.

Gerald remembered an almighty row round about half term. He'd been in his room sketchily designing what he imagined would be the car of the future when he heard the raised voices and the slamming doors. His father had recently explained to him in a confidential way that he would have a new baby brother or sister before the end of the year but seemingly his mother was not hugely delighted with this situation. Her figure, her looks, her ambitions would be in ruins. The atmosphere was heavy with resentment. In spite of his weighty misgivings Father had agreed to a final late-year excursion on the new cruiser. It had become final in a way no-one had imagined.

Gerald did his best to fit in with life in his new home. His uncle was a chartered surveyor and, as his cousin Jack boasted, made 'pots of money'. They enjoyed outdoor activities as a family, going on weekend hikes and camping trips with Uncle Arnold mildly protesting that he was too old for the rigours of the countryside. Gradually Gerald thought less and less about his early life. He did exceptionally well at Senior school and went on to study architecture. On his twenty-first birthday he suddenly became very wealthy inheriting the money from his parents' estate.

Now, almost twenty years on from the time of the disaster, he felt ready to go back to the Island. He had no large scale projects that

114

could not be dealt with by partners in the firm and his latest relationship had gone the way of so many others. Commitment was something from which he shrank and girls got tired of indecision.

It was summer. He had a brand new BMW xDrive 40d and a booking on the Island ferry for the coming Friday. His intention was to pass some time in Edinburgh en route in order to cast a professional eye over the Parliamentary building which had caused so much controversy at the time of its completion.

Gerald's rooms in the Island capital's most prominent hotel were much to his satisfaction and a friendly chat with the girl on reception gave him the details he needed to find the little village the following day.

Nothing seemed familiar as he drove through but he had been very young and confused at the time of the boating tragedy. Only the village's General Stores jogged his memory a little. He had a vague recollection of a stocky man with a bristling moustache, a very no-nonsense type, and his wife a smiling woman in a flowered overall who had given him sweets. The shop bell pinged above his head as he made to enter. A customer was on his way out pocketing some change and calling a cheerio. Gerald held the door for him.

"Thank you very much," the man said. "My that's a grand motor you have." He smiled. "You could carry a fair lot of peats home in that."

Gerald perished the thought and moved towards the counter where a stern-faced woman in a buttoned-up green overall was eyeing him expectantly. Another in identical garb was monitoring two small children as they investigated the contents of the ice cream freezer. What he took to be the mother was selecting 'local views' from the squeaky stand which displayed the postcards. It was uncomfortably hot. He decided he'd need to buy something in order to engage the shop-lady in conversation.

"I'll have these please." He placed two bottles of high-energy drink on the counter. Pleasantries regarding the weather were exchanged before Gerald explained the reason behind his visit. Yes, the lady remembered the awful accident. "It was my parents who'd have kept the shop at that time, both gone now." Dollag MacSween told him. Gerald muttered sympathetically. He asked about the coastguard and was told he too was no longer with them, and his wife, frail and confused, was in residential care in the town.

"No, it would be unlikely that she would remember you. Twenty five pence change, thank you." Gerald felt he had been dismissed.

The younger woman came over, wiping her hands on a paper towel. "Oh but I'm sure I mind on you coming in here with Rhoda. She bought you a pair of Wellingtons; Fergus's ones were huge on you. Fergus is still here – the son – lives down by the harbour. He's a prawn fisher." Peigi was enjoying being the helpful informant. "You'll easily know the house; there's a model lighthouse and a lot of boats and things in the front yard. He makes them when he can't get out to sea."

Down at the pier Gerald found Fergus mending creels in the shade of a lean-to shed. It wasn't easy to think what to say; he did his best to explain himself as briefly as possible. Fergus looked him up and down cannily before extending his hand to the younger man.

"By jove, that was a while ago." He grinned. "I remember being a bit annoyed having to share my room with the little English stranger. My mother gave you stuff of mine to wear and it was all far too big. What have you been doing with yourself since that time? Come on in the house and I'll brew up … unless you'd prefer something stronger?"

Gerald shook his head, indicating the parked BMW. Fergus whistled in admiration.

Gerald spoke of the unusual building he had passed on the way down; he'd noticed the Property Agent's 'For Sale' sign.

"It's been on the market since October last year after old Isa MacDonald passed away. The extension next to it was a sail loft in the olden days – that's why it's so long. It would need quite a bit of work. There's nobody in these parts could afford to buy it. The young folk mostly have to move away from the area. Are you thinking of putting in an offer?" he added jokingly.

"I doubt that," Gerald replied. "But I'll likely be back down here again; I'm on a fortnight's holiday. There's so much I want to see of this beautiful part of the world."

"Oh well, if you were here on a bleak November day with the wind taking the feet from you and the rain blattering down you might think differently. It should stay like this for a day or two yet; the forecast wasn't bad. Don't expect much happening tomorrow, it's the Sunday. You'll be all right up in town as long as you're not looking for a swim or a round of golf."

116

'I could get used to these full Scottish breakfasts,' mused Gerald as he headed the powerful car south to the site of the famous Standing Stones. Fergus had been right about the weather holding. Over the weekend Gerald's thoughts had gone back time and again to the empty building by the harbour. A stunning location, the asking price probably well below English standards. It would be ideal for something like flats to fill the gap in the affordable housing market. He would telephone the Estate Agent later in the day and arrange a viewing.

Perhaps he could give something back to the small community where he had been shown such kindness and at the same time leave a lasting tribute to the memory of his father and mother in the tragic place where they had lost their lives.